It Looked Like A
SOFT TOUCH . . .

A beautiful bride, an interest in her old man's business, and a salary too big for the job.

But that was before my wife turned into a lush. And before the business started to go to pieces.

Before Vince Biskay rang my bell and cased my situation real fast. He knew I'd be ripe for almost any proposition—and it didn't take him long to find out Lorraine was ripe too, in her own special way.

JOHN D. MacDONALD

SOFT TOUCH

A FAWCETT GOLD MEDAL BOOK

Fawcett Publications, Inc., Greenwich, Conn.
Member of American Book Publishers Council, Inc.

SOFT TOUCH

Chapter 1

When I got home at six o'clock on an April Friday, the first hot day of the year, Lorraine's copper-colored Porsche was parked crooked in the driveway, keys in the ignition. After I put the station wagon in the garage, I ran hers in.

I went into the kitchen. She could be in the house or she could be somewhere in the neighborhood acquiring her evening edge. There was no point in yelling. If she didn't feel like answering, she wouldn't answer. And say later she hadn't heard a thing.

A man should like to come home at night. It had been a long time since I had looked forward to coming home. And this was the worst day of all. For the eight childless years I have been married to her, I have worked for her father, E. J. Malton of the E. J. Malton Construction Company—a little white-skinned man with a face like a trout and a voice like a French horn—one of those completely terrifying little men who combine arrogant stupidity with a devout conviction of their own infallibility.

I didn't know then that this was the night Vince Biskay was going to show up out of the past, a tiger in the night, a tiger coming to call, offering the silky temptation of big violent money. And if I'd known how it was going to work out for me, I would never have come home that night. Or any other night.

But I went dutifully into the dull house at 118 Tyler Drive, the eight-year-old wedding present from her parents, and I found her in the bedroom, sitting at her dressing table in yellow bra and panties, doing her nails, half of an old fashioned handy at her elbow.

7

She gave me a quick glance in the mirror and said, "Hi."

I sat on the foot of my bed and said, "What's up?"

"What do you mean, what's up? Does something have to be up?"

"I thought maybe you were getting fixed up to go out."

"I'm doing my nails. Obviously."

"Are we going out?"

"Who said we were going out? Irene's going to get dinner."

"She wasn't down there when I came in."

"So maybe she went to the john in the cellar. How should I know? She didn't clue me."

"All right, Lorrie, all right. I've got the picture. You're doing your nails. We're eating in. And did you have a happy, happy day?"

"It was so warm Mandy had her gardener fill the pool. But the water was too stinking cold."

By then I could tell how slopped she was. Not too bad. The one at her elbow was probably her third. Two years after we were married the drinking began to turn from a habit into a problem. A problem she still won't admit. I don't know why she drinks. The too simple answer is that she's unhappy. She's married to me. So part of the blame belongs to me.

We got that adoption thing all lined up once, four years ago. But Lorraine, just before it went through, ran drunk through a stop sign and piled up the MG and got that little scar at the corner of her pretty mouth, and had her license lifted and I paid the two-hundred-dollar fine. The adoption people canceled us out. And I haven't suggested we try again. Nor will I.

I watched her and again felt astonished that the heavy drinking has left no mark on her. She is a damned attractive female. They spoiled her and spoiled her brother rotten, and so she is unhappy, shallow, lazy, short-tempered, cruel and amoral. Yet sometimes there is a sweetness . . . So rarely. Once in a rare, rare while we are very good together, and when it is good it is like a beginning, and you can kid yourself into thinking the marriage will improve. But it won't.

I went to her and put my hands on her bare shoulders, my thumbs on the soft nape of her neck. She shrugged my hands away irritably. "For God's sake, Jerry."

"Just a thought."

"Aren't you getting enough from Liz down at the office?"

"You know that's nonsense," I said. I sat on the bed again and lighted a cigarette. I had to tell her how the only good part of my little world had just come to a dirty end.

"Today, Lorrie, your old man took over Park Terrace."

"So?"

"Maybe you could try hard to understand. He promised me a free hand. It's the biggest development the company has ever gotten into. I've worked like a dog for months and months so we'd put up some expensive spec houses we can move. It isn't a seller's market any more. Now he's changed his mind and he's going to put up one hundred homes just as dull as this one, the same house he's been building for years. And it will be a fiasco and everything will go down the drain. Everything he owns and we own."

She turned around on the bench and looked at me coldly. "You know so damn much, Jerry. Daddy has gotten along fine. And he'll keep on getting along just fine."

"A lot of stupid men have done fine in a business way. Good luck and good timing. He's run out of luck this time. He took it away from me today. All that work down the drain. So . . . I'm getting out."

Her eyes widened. "Just how do you expect to do that?"

"I don't know. I'll need some capital to get going on my own again. Sell our stock back to the corporation. Unload this crumby house to somebody who's impressed by the neighborhood."

"The house is in our names, and I won't sign a thing.

This is all a lot of talk. You won't get out. You couldn't make a living."

But I had made a living, before I met her. After I got out of the army in that second war, I had the restless itch. I had done some roving and some roaming, and I had gotten into several kinds of choice trouble—bigger trouble than the kind I had gotten into in high school and my two years of college. The trouble hadn't scared me at all until one day I found myself in a Reno motel with a small group of deadly chums and we were planning how we would knock over one of the casinos. I'd been hypnotized by all those heavy stacks of money. And that scared me good and so I'd come home to Vernon, taken some odd jobs and then, on money borrowed from my mother the year before she died, money that was all that was left of my father's small estate, I had drifted sideways into home construction. Jerry Jamison, Builder. And I liked it. I learned the trade. I did well at it.

Until, at a contractors' picnic, I met Lorraine Malton, fresh out of college, in July of 1957. She was with her father, E. J. I had met him a few times and thought him tiresome, self-important, and not very bright. But I had never seen anything more delightful than Lorrie. Glossy black hair and eyes of a wonderful clear blue. She wore white sharkskin shorts that day and a yellow blouse, and her legs were a longness of honey and velvet. When she moved it was like dancing, her narrow waist emphasizing the dainty abundancies that kept her constantly encircled by all the unattached men at the picnic. She had a cute squinty grin and no time for me at all.

I guess I was ready to be married. I campaigned hard. Perhaps if I hadn't been so eager I might have been able to see her more clearly, see the petulance and the greediness and the drinking. She had been brought up to believe she was the most important person in the world. And the verve that all pretty young girls possess kept her basic character from showing itself too clearly.

So we were married on the fifteenth day of August, and, after an unforgettably strenuous Bermuda honeymoon, we moved into the wedding present house a block away from her parents. The week after we returned the thriving little business of Jerry Jamison, Builder, was absorbed by a stock deal into the E. J. Malton Construction Company, along with my good work crew foremanned by Red Olin. I got some stock and I became General Manager at twenty thousand a year. Both Lorrie and her brother, Eddie, Junior, then nineteen, had been given small blocks of stock. Eddie was a slack, dim, acne-ridden young man.

I had it the best. I was vigorous, with a gorgeous, lusty and loving wife. The corporation was stagnant, but I was going to make the old flooph see the light and start to wheel and deal in some modern house construction.

And that was only eight years ago. And now I was forty-three, with the house, some cash value in insurance, and eleven hundred bucks in the joint checking account—if Lorraine hadn't been shopping today. During the eight years the dividends on the stock had been too liberal. E. J. enjoyed passing out checks at Christmas. And both Lorrie and her mother had one approach to money—if it was there, spend it.

"I'm going to get out," I told her.

She turned her back, huffed on her nails and then began to brush her hair. "You're boring me, Jerry. Honestly you are. You won't get out. Go take your shower or something."

As I was wondering how it would feel to spin her around and bust her solidly in the mouth, I heard the front door chimes.

"Who the hell would that be?" I asked.

"And how the hell would I know? Go answer it."

I went down and opened the front door. A man as tall as I am stood there, and the familiar grin was wide and strong.

"Vince!" I said. "You bastard! My God, come in."

He came in, and he put his suitcase down in the hall, and we pumped hands and thumped shoulders and he said, still grinning, "Greetings, lieutenant."

The last time I had seen Vince was in Calcutta in August of 1945, twenty years ago. As my air transportation home had lifted off the runway I had looked down and seen him for the last time. He was standing beside the borrowed jeep between the two White Russian girls with whom we had spent the past two weeks, and he was drinking from a bottle and waving at the same time.

I could see at once that he had weathered the years a little better than I had. He was deeply tanned and his grip was hard and firm. He is a big man, and something about his cat-lazy way of moving, his air of potential recklessness, has always reminded me of that Mitchum in the movies. Vince has a square jaw, high hard round cheekbones, and an odd slanting flatness about his eyes. There was a subtly foreign flavor about the cut of his suit, the trim of his hair, the large red stone in the gold ring on the little finger of his right hand.

"I shall build drinks," I said, "and you will become a house guest."

"What else?" he said, and followed me out into the kitchen to lounge against a counter top and watch me.

Vince Biskay and I had achieved a special closeness during the war. We met when we were both assigned to Operations in O.S.S. Detachment 404 operating out of Ceylon under Lord Louis's headquarters. Operations behind Jap lines had required a special kind of go-to-hell talent, and I suspect we were prime examples of what was needed. We worked well together. So we were sent together on one extended and three short operations, accompanied only by native agents. That was our war. A pretty nervous war, at times. You can lie on your face in the jungle brush and hear the Jap patrol clink and jangle by on the trail eight feet away from you, and when they are out of earshot, you can throw up because you've been that scared. Captain Biskay was in charge every time. We found out what they sent us to find out and radioed the data back to the Trinco tower. We destroyed what we could, and we armed the ones who wanted to fight. And I learned a lot they never taught me at Benning.

And now, twenty years later, he was in my kitchen and we clinked two strong Scotch and waters together, and I asked him how long he'd managed to stay in Calcutta after I left.

"A couple of weeks more, I think. Then I had to get out while I had my health."

"You had my address. Not one damn postcard in twenty years."

"I didn't say I'd write."

"What are you doing in Vernon?"

He held his glass up to the light. "Came to visit, old pal. Came to see you."

"You look prosperous enough. What have you been doing?"

"Many many things, Jerry."

"Married?"

"I tried it. I didn't like it."

He was being almost rudely evasive, yet I got the impression that he was studying me with great care. I could sense that he was under some kind of strain. He was just a little too relaxed, and I remembered that that was the way he had always been when we had something laid on and we were getting close to the time for jump-off.

Lorraine came into the kitchen bearing her empty glass, wearing her maroon tailored doeskin slacks and a white orlon blouse.

"I heard you talking to . . ." Then she saw Vince and said, "Oh! How do you do?"

"Honey, this is the fabulous Vince Biskay, the legendary guy I've told you about. My wife Lorraine, Vince."

I saw her react to him. I had seen a lot of women react to Vince. I felt a little twist of jealousy as I saw the heightened color, a shine in the eyes, a flirtatiousness in the smile, a barely perceptible arching of the back.

They went through the so-nice-to-meet-you routine. I built Lorraine a new drink. I was very jolly, doing the happy-marriage bit. Even as I was doing it, I knew it was off key. A good marriage has a distinctive and unmistakable flavor. It can't be faked. There is a warmth about it. When it is a marriage of strangers, no affectionate gestures, no amount of folksy enthusiasm can delude the discerning observer. And I was certain that

13

Vince, with that almost feminine intuition of his, sensed the drabness and sourness of our relationship.

When I alerted Lorraine to the fact that Vince had his suitcase with him and would stay with us, she responded with unexpected enthusiasm. She usually avoids all house guests. She became the jolly hostess, and took Vince up to show him the better of the two guest rooms where he would stay.

I went back out into the kitchen and told Irene there would be three for dinner. She is a drab and faded woman, so deeply and emotionally concerned with her relationship to her church that she seems remote to everything else in the world. She is a good cook and housekeeper.

I went into the living room and I heard Vince and Lorrie coming down the stairs. I heard Lorrie laugh. It was her social laugh, the one she uses when she's being particularly charming. But there was an added texture to it, a throaty sexuality.

Lorraine was very vivacious during dinner, dominating the conversation. But immediately after dinner she began to sag in the familiar way. Her eyes went dull and her diction went to hell and she could not follow the conversation. At about ten o'clock she gave us a glassy good night and went wobbling off to bed, precariously carrying her bedside jolt of raw brandy.

"And now," I said to Vince, "you can tell me what's on your mind."

Chapter 2

We settled into the breakfast booth off the kitchen with fresh drinks. Irene had cleaned up and gone home. The back door was open and the first bugs of the season were banging their heads against the screen.

He smiled at me in a wry, wise way. "Old Jamison. Now you carry a Chamber of Commerce card."

"Junior chamber."

"And you're all settled down. Maybe you're too far settled down for . . . this little thing I have in mind."

"So try and see."

"First, I'm in the country illegally. I'm not a citizen anymore. I've got a very good passport. Forged. My boss thinks I'm off on a hunting trip in Brazil. He'd get nervous if he knew I was in the States. He might even figure out what I've got on my mind. Something I've been thinking about for months. Two good men can swing it. Me, and somebody I can trust. Really trust. So I keep thinking of you, Jerry."

"Aren't you sort of backing into this?"

He grinned and became more direct. He told me he had adopted nationality. For reasons which will become obvious, I will call that country Valencia. It is a country in South America under a strong dictatorial thumb.

"The things I tried after the war didn't work out, Jerry. I was too restless. I got a license to fly. And then I decided to blow what was left of my father's estate in buying a plane and taking a tour of Central and South America. I had a ball for about a year. I began to run thin in the money department in Valencia. I met a man at a party. I told him the shape I was in. He took my hotel address and said he had an idea. The next day a driver came and picked me up in a fat Mercedes and took me out to be interviewed by a Señor Melendez way the hell and gone out in the country at his ranch. He wanted a man for odd jobs, a pilot with both English and Spanish, somebody who wouldn't get alarmed if things might get a little rough now and then.

"I went to work for him eight years ago. It's been . . . very interesting, Jerry. As tests he set up certain . . . temptations in my path. But I was just shrewd enough to play it his way. So, insofar as Melendez trusts anybody he trusts Vincente Biskay. And it's been profitable.

"Outside of our semi-benevolent dictator, el General Peral, Melendez is the most powerful man in the country. He's an industrialist. Never has operated in the political field. A cold and ruthless guy. Now we come to the meat. For the past three years Peral and Melendez have been moving toward a showdown. Through monkeying with the tax structure, Peral has been putting the squeeze on Melendez. Raoul Melendez has been getting too strong and powerful, and any dictator gets nervous when one of his subjects shows signs of getting too damn big. Peral has been trying to clip his wings. Raoul Melendez won't stand for it. So, to keep from being sunk without a trace, he's forced to go into the field of political action. And in that area, it means bullets. Follow me?"

"Who is going to win, Vince?"

"Pertinent question. I think Peral is the likely one. He has the hard core of the professional army in his pocket. Melendez has bought himself some young and ambitious army officers. They've been selected with great care, but I can't be certain Peral hasn't got a plant among them. Melendez has been planning the coup with great care. It is supposed to look like a spontaneous uprising of the people and a chunk of the army to depose Peral. If it's successful the country will be governed by an army junta for a time, and then a man will go in as boss man and he will be one of Melendez's tame ones. But I don't think the dream will work. And if it shouldn't work and I don't get out in time, I might get some mortal knots on my head. So, I'm making other plans. It's a horse race and I'm betting Peral on the nose."

"How?"

He took a long pull at his drink and set the glass down empty. "I've got a special source of information very close to Raoul Melendez. Very damn close. In bed with him, in fact. She has a lively intelligence and a lot of curiosity, and a deft way of getting data out of Melendez. Melendez is stockpiling modern weapons for the great day. In a recent fracas in the Middle East, one country picked up a lot of stuff they didn't need. They've put it on the open market. The top agent for it is a smart Greek named Kyodos who lives in the States. He likes dollars. He has good shipping line contacts. So Raoul

Melendez has been converting his holdings in other South American countries into U. S. dollars and turning them over to Kyodos. In return some very effective infantry weapons, some light artillery and some light armored vehicles are being landed right under Peral's nose, marked as machinery and equipment for one of Melendez's new industrial construction projects. It gets stockpiled at a remote hacienda, and one of my recent projects has been to train the willing peons in the use thereof. The flow is still going on. It's a slow process because it takes time to accumulate enough dollars to make a respectable shipment of funds to Kyodos. It just so happens, ole buddy, that I know exactly how the next wad of currency is being shipped and exactly when. Does any light dawn?"

"So far I'm not interested."

"Didn't expect you to be. You're a moral type. My deal with Carmela, Melendez's tootsie, involves getting her out from under. Plus a share of the take. But not a big share. The big share is for me. And you."

"I don't feel any reaction yet."

"It would not be theft, Jerry. Keep that in mind. It would be just a little job of hijacking the war funds of a greedy joker who is trying to overturn the stable and U.S.-recognized government in what promises to be a very bloody-type revolution. Hundreds of innocents killed. From the moral viewpoint we'd be doing the world a favor."

"Not 'we,' Vince. This sounds crazy to me. Listening to it in my own kitchen makes it sound crazier."

"At great personal risk, but with certain . . . pleasant compensations, I have been teaching the lovely Carmela to fly a plane. She only has to make one trip. And by the time it's over, Melendez won't be coming after her, because by that time he'll be in one of Peral's nice deep political prisons, or maybe a few feet deeper than that. Here's how easy it will be, Jerry. I get out at precisely the right time to meet you at Tampa. With a plan I've devised, which takes two to handle it, we deftly remove the funds from the courier. At about the same time that is happening, Carmela is taking off, having made certain the complete plans of the whole operation are falling into Peral's hands. The Melendez empire goes pfft, we arrange our split and part forever. Nobody is hurt. No agitated forces of law and order. Nobody in any shape to claim anything stolen. I need one other man to swing it, a man I can trust."

I tried to think of the right way to say it. He got up to fix himself a drink. I said, "Maybe we've grown apart in twenty years, Vince. I'm not the same kind of guy I was then. I can't even imagine myself capable of doing some of the things I did then, taking some of the risks. You can call me stuffy, but you're operating out of my league. I wouldn't want to take a chance of getting all jammed up like that even if there was . . . oh, a hundred thousand bucks in it for me. I'm just a businessman in a medium-sized city. I used to do risky things, but that was a war. You're still living that way, Vince, but I'm not."

As he sat down opposite me he looked thoughtful. "Boy, are you leading the big warm happy life? There's never been any kids in this house."

"That's beside the point."

"No it isn't. If the setup looked good, then maybe this would have been just a friendly visit. Your lady is a lush, friend."

"That's beside the point too."

"I'll ask a different kind of question. What do you think war matériel costs in this brave new world anyway?"

"Quite a lot probably."

"Melendez is worth somewhere between a third and a half billion dollars, Jerry. So he's investing maybe forty million in his venture into politics. And, my naïve friend, in the next shipment of funds to Kyodos there will be between three and a quarter and three and three quarters millions of dollars. Untraceable. Nobody will be anxious to claim it. The Greek won't come after it. Melendez will be sunk. Peral will have no interest. The joker we take it away from will certainly make no squawk to the authorities. It's a once in a dozen lifetimes chance, laddy.

You're forty-three now. The split goes this way. I get two. You get one. Carmela gets the overage up to a half million. Anything over that you and I split down the middle. Your minimum will be one, your probable maximum one million one hundred and twenty-five thousand. But it could run to one million three. Then you have your choice. You can try to put it to work here without exciting the interest of the little men with the briefcases. Or you can become an expatriate and live in horrible luxurious indolence for the rest of your turn around the track. We planned a lot of cute things together, Jerry, and we pulled them all off and, believe me, this little hassle is simple as can be compared with some of those others. So don't say no in too big a hurry. Think it over. Mind if I carry this one up to my bed?"

After he had gone up, I made myself some coffee. I sat in the booth for a long time. I thought of certain small changes in Vince. There had been a lightness in him that was now deadened. I sensed a coldness. But, hell, I had changed too. I wasn't exactly bursting with joy. For the past two years young Eddie had been working for E. J. Malton, and at more pay than he deserved. His willingness to try to give me orders indicated that in his own mind he was the heir apparent. I suspected that if E. J. kicked off, young Eddie would inherit papa's stock which, along with mama's, would give him effective control. And working with the kid would be impossible, if there was any company left.

One million dollars. Freedom from E. J. Maybe freedom from Lorraine too. Because I had had just about enough.

And I found myself wondering if I might make room for Liz Addams. E. J. had hired her three years ago. The widow of a naval aviator, she had bought secretarial training with his insurance money. A tall, gray-eyed gal with pale, lustrous, creamy hair and a very direct manner. No coy feminine antics, and a good sense of humor. I had liked her from the beginning. About a year ago, for no reason at all, Lorraine started needling me about Liz. And only then did I begin to look at Liz from a different point of view—and see the curve of her waist, and the tilt of a hip, the long trim legs, and the soft and generous look of her lips.

And I started to daydream about her a little bit.

And took her to coffee and worked the conversation around to Lorraine's accusations. Liz was amused and a little bit angry. "Buster," she said. "May I call you Buster? If the next step in this little gambit is to tell me we've got the name, so let's have the game, the answer is no. No office romances for Lizzie."

"I wasn't thinking of just an ordinary romance," I told her. "I was thinking of fleeing together to Samarkand or Pago Pago."

"Or Scranton. Let's get back to work."

So now I daydreamed a little more. I added Liz to the million bucks and came up with an island, house boys, a schooner at anchor, and Liz swimming in the sunlight in the coral lagoon. . . .

But that was nonsense. I could be grateful to Vince for one reason. His wild plan had increased my determination to get out of E. J.'s little family corporation. Seeing Vince had crystallized my discontent with a futile job and a spoiled child wife.

Your lady is a lush. It had made me angry when he said that in his cold, amused way. But it was accurate.

Maybe this was the time to get out. Change the dice once more before it was too late.

I went up to bed. There was no need to be quiet. I could have marched Armstrong and all the saints through the bedroom without changing the deep drugged rhythm of her breathing. I stood over her and looked at the slack sleeping face. In sleep her face had the innocence and vulnerability of a child's.

After I was in bed I began to plan my little chat with E. J.

Chapter 3

Liz told me at nine o'clock Saturday morning that the big little man wasn't in yet. It was raining steadily. The rain on the window by her desk had a stained and greasy look.

I sat by her desk and said, "I suppose he sent out a lot of cancellations when he got back yesterday."

"Dozens. All by wire."

"Liz, I'm going to get out."

She finished a line of her typing, banged the carriage back and turned and looked at me. "It's about time, Jerry."

"I didn't know what your reaction would be. I didn't expect that."

"Why not? Couldn't it be as obvious to me as it is to you? All your reasons?" She glanced toward the door and said, "Good morning, Mr. Malton."

E. J. came in, followed closely by Eddie. "Good morning, good morning, good morning! Great day for ducks."

"I want to talk to you, E. J."

"In a moment, Jerry. In a moment." And he went into his office with Junior and shut the door. Junior didn't come out for half an hour. I couldn't imagine any conversation that would require his presence for half an hour.

"Come in, Jerry," E. J. baroomed.

I shut the door behind me. I sat down and said, "I want you to listen to me, E. J. To what I say."

"You know perfectly well I give my full attention to everything that comes up."

"I chickened out yesterday, E. J. I let you bluff me. You went ahead and canceled the orders I placed."

"Orders you placed after revising working drawings without my permission. You know the rules around here."

21

"I want a showdown. I want those houses built my way. You promised me a free hand."

"A free hand within the rules. *Within* our operating procedures."

"Nuts. Do you let me build them my way?"

"On a project this big, Jerry, I'd be a damn fool to let you go ahead with a lot of silly experimentation. If you're asking a stupid question, the answer is no."

"Then I want out. Now."

"Why, if we were to go ahead with your ideas, we'd be the laughing . . . What did you just say?"

"I said I want out."

"Out of the corporation? You want to be released?"

"More than just a release. I've got two hundred shares of stock in my own name, E. J. When I came in eight years ago, Dan Dentry kept telling me I was making a good deal. Okay, then it should work both ways. I have here a complete inventory of everything you picked up out of my little business. On a conservative estimate of value, I've worked it out at eight thousand dollars. So you can have my two hundred shares back for eight thousand bucks, E. J., and we'll shake hands and you can stop scrapping with me."

For once he was really listening. He pursed his trout-mouth and said, "Absolutely impossible, Jerry. I'm disappointed at your attitude. We have our little dissensions, but I thought we were a good team. You certainly know that the size of this project requires all the working capital we can swing."

"If the corporation can't buy the shares back, suppose you buy them personally."

"I'm in no position to do that."

"Then give me a truck and some tools up to eight thousand dollars' worth."

"Park Terrace will require all the equipment we have."

"Can you get it through your thick head that I'm through?"

"I can understand you're being rude and stupid."

"You won't make any kind of deal on the stock?"

"No."

I stood up. "I'm still through."

"And you are still my son-in-law, Jerry. You can do as you please. If and when your attitude changes, I can always make a place for you here."

"You think this firm will go on forever?"

"I see no reason why it should fail."

I caught Cal Warder at his desk at the Merchants Midland Bank a little after ten o'clock. We made some golf talk and then I gave him the story. But Cal had been doing a little investigating of his own regarding E. J. Malton. He is a nice guy but he had the banker's instinct for a sorry situation. He thought he might get a loan of a thousand dollars on my two hundred shares past his loan committee, but he wouldn't guarantee anything. We made a rough balance sheet of my assets. I told him Lorraine wouldn't let me unload the house. All he could offer me was his sympathy, and advice to go back with E. J. and try to stave off disaster.

I thanked him for laying it on the line. I got home at eleven. Vince was in the living room, leafing through a magazine. He said Irene had fixed him a good breakfast and he thought Lorrie was up because he had heard her shower running a little while ago.

I went up. She was in the bathroom drying herself on a big yellow towel and humming to herself. I hadn't heard so much cheer in months. I looked around the bedroom and the bathroom, but I didn't spot a morning jolt anywhere.

"Good morning, darling," she said. "What are you doing home so early? Don't you trust me alone with your exciting friend?"

I followed her into the bedroom and sat on the dressing table bench and watched her select panties and step into them and snap the elastic across her stomach.

"I'm home because I'm unemployed. I quit this morning."

She stared at me. "You must be out of your mind."

"I've got good reasons, but let's not go into them. The fact remains, I quit. Your old man won't buy my stock

23

back. I've got to have money. I don't think we've talked seriously in a long time, Lorraine. Or hardly talked at all. Now I'm talking seriously. I'm asking . . . begging for your co-operation. I want to put this dismal house on the market and price it to move. We can move into a rental deal for a while. I can get Red Olin back and some good men for a working crew. With decent capital, I don't think it will take me too long to get healthy."

She didn't answer. I could not read her expression. She slipped her arms into bra straps, then bent forward from the waist to hammock her breasts neatly, straightened up and snapped the fastening. She took a cigarette from her night stand and lit it. She looked at me.

"Now I'm convinced you're out of your mind."

"Lorraine, all I'm asking—"

"—is for me to make a choice between you and my family, Jerry. All over some stupid little quarrel we had yesterday."

"It isn't only that."

"That's all there is to it. Now let me tell you something. You're trying to force me into a choice. All right. If you keep it up, I'll choose my family. Gladly. Gratefully. I won't even saddle you with any alimony, dear. I'll take a settlement, thank you. This house, both cars, the checking account, and three thousand dollars in cash. And, of course, your stock in the company. If you want to be stubborn, dear, I'll strip you just as naked as you were when Daddy took you on and started paying you more than you've ever been worth, or ever will be."

"You're so damn easy to get along with, Lorraine."

"Now you've got the choice, darling. It's right in your lap."

She went to her closet to select clothing. I was tempted to tell her she'd made herself a deal. But a little whisper of wariness drifted through my mind. If I said what I had intended to say, I'd have to pack and get out. And perhaps, for Vince's purposes, the house was a base.

"You make it tough," I said.

"No tougher than you want to make it on me." She

zipped her skirt, turned from side to side to look at herself in her mirror.

"I guess I better do some more thinking."

"I guess you should."

When she went downstairs I did some more thinking. I sat there a long time. I uncapped a couple of bottles of her scent and sniffed them, and wondered what they had cost per ounce. How many gallons could you get for a million bucks? Or would it be simpler to buy the distillery or whatever you called the place where they made perfume?

When I went down I heard her laughing that laugh again. The one that wasn't for me. The one that was for Vince.

When I walked into the dining room where she was being served breakfast and Vince was being served more coffee, she said, "And here comes the brave and fearless unemployed one. Did he tell you yet? He quit his job this morning. He quit Daddy in a monstrous huff."

I saw the quick look of interest in Vince's eyes. "It won't be too much trouble to line something else up," I said. "Her old man is a practicing psychopath. He finally wore me out."

"Daddy is a dreamboat," she said demurely, and as I looked at her I wondered why this should be the first time I noticed that her mouth did have, in much less degree, that same look of the trout.

It took some doing to pry Lorraine loose from Vince. On the pretext that I was going to show him some houses I had built, I drove him out to the Helena Forest Road and parked in one of the state picnic places. The rain was coming down harder.

"What does it mean that you quit your job?" he asked, turning in the seat so he was facing me.

"Not what you might think. I've got other plans, Vince."

"Oh."

"But—just for the hell of it, understand—I'd like a little more detail on this nice smooth operation in Tampa."

"Just for the hell of it. Okay. As a courier Melendez

25

is using a regular diplomatic courier from another South American country. Melendez owns this boy body and soul. I've never met him, but I've studied some very clear and accurate photographs of him. He makes his next trip on either the seventh or eighth of May, from the capital of his country to the office of his country's consul in Tampa. He will have diplomatic immunity from customs search. This will be his fourth trip bearing money. The procedure will be the same. He will be met at the Tampa International Airport by an official car with uniformed chauffeur and one other passenger. It is possible that he may be under surveillance by Kyodos's people from the moment he lands. In the past the car has stopped at a downtown hotel. He registers and takes his suitcase to the room. Then he returns to the official car and takes the pouch to the consulate. While he is at the consulate, Kyodos's people pick up the money from the hotel room. I don't know just how that is arranged, but it isn't important."

"Is this a daylight deal?"

"Yes. I wouldn't risk any kind of an operation after the money is in Kyodos's possession. That Greek is too smart and too rough. We have to make the interception between the airport and the hotel."

"Oh, dandy!" I said. "Armed robbery by daylight right in the middle of traffic."

"Jerry boy, you are losing your touch. Have you ever known me to be crude? Here is the way I've worked it out. You will arrive in Tampa on the sixth and register at the Tampa Terrace Hotel. I will have gotten there earlier. By then I will know the exact flight he'll be on and the time. And I'll have made certain other arrangements. I will have available a nice black sedan, rented or purchased, and in either case very discreetly. And I will have a gray chauffeur's uniform that will fit you perfectly. Or perfectly enough."

"Oh, no!"

"Don't let your little heart go pitter-patter. In plenty of time before his flight arrives, the consulate will be advised by cable that he will arrive on a later flight. I will meet him in the terminal, and my Spanish is excellent, Jerry. I will have a plausible cover story which need not worry you. You will be in the car and it will be parked in such a way he will not be likely to see the plates. I've already acquired a nice little official decal for the side of the door. Believe me, he will come along like a lamb."

"And if he doesn't?"

"Have confidence in Uncle Vince. And if he doesn't, where do you stand? Have you done anything illegal?"

"Go ahead."

"By then you will have been over the route at least twice, more if he doesn't come until the eighth. At the very first opportunity, I will quiet the gentleman with my little bag of shot. And then stick him with enough demerol for a four-hour nap. Then we will be alert to see if we are being followed by Kyodos's people. If not, we take the car to a downtown lot where you can park it yourself. And lock it. The gentleman will be on the floor in back, snug under a blanket, with his head pillowed on his diplomatic pouch."

"And if we are followed?"

"You do look on the dark side of things, Jerry. In that remote possibility, I have an alternate plan. We drive directly to the emergency entrance of a hospital I have selected. In voluble and excited broken English I ask help for the unfortunate gentleman who passed out without reason. We accompany him into the hospital, with baggage. It will baffle the people tailing us. They will have no special reason to suspect we are not legitimate, unless they get clever about the plates. You will go out a side entrance to a cab stand, carrying the suitcase of money. I will say I must take the pouch to the consulate. I will park the car in the lot as in Plan A, leave the pouch therein, lose myself in the labyrinth of a handy department store and join you at the hotel. And within an hour we will be out of town."

"How?"

"We can decide that later."

"If you have to buy the car, why not use that?"

27

"We might do it that way. Any flaws?"

"In the hospital bit. I don't like wandering around with a chauffeur's uniform on. And going in and out of the hotel."

"People look at the uniform, not the face. An air of casual confidence and professional deference is all you will need. At one point you will have the money all to yourself—in Plan B. That's why I had to select an associate with great care."

"I can understand that. What if the cable gets fouled up and two cars show at the airport?"

"That detail won't be fouled up."

"Will you carry a gun?"

"Why?"

"I don't think I'd like the sound of it if you do."

"I don't see why I would need one."

"Then don't."

"Anything to please you. I take it you've agreed."

"Did I say that?"

"No, but you sound as if you're going along."

"I've got to think about it."

"There's also Plan C, which I've been giving consideration to. Drive right out of town with our pigeon. Give him a second shot when he starts to come around. Keep moving. But that keeps us in the car too long. It increases the possibility of the things you can't plan for. Speeding ticket. Accident. Breakdown. I say we dump the car fast, and him too."

"Sounds better."

"It would be easier at night. But it will be a daylight arrival. I've checked the possible flights. PanAm 675 at three-fifteen on the afternoon of the seventh looks most likely. If so, at three o'clock lots will be happening. Peral will be reading his mail and Carmela will be making a nervous solo."

"When do we divide it and split up?"

"I don't want to hang around Tampa long enough to do that."

"Where do we go?"

"I suggest we take a bus to Clearwater, check in at

28

a downtown hotel, transact our business and split up in the morning."

"It isn't like Burma."

"The general philosophy is the same. There's just more people."

"Wouldn't it make a hell of a lot more sense if I brought a car down there?"

"I thought of that. I didn't go into it thoroughly. I didn't think you'd want to take too much time off."

"Time off from what?"

"You have a point."

"It might make a cleaner job. Leave the hospital part in. My wagon will be parked near that cab stand you talked about. I just go out and get in it. Then I go wait near the department store. And we go on from there, Clearwater or any place else."

"That's clear thinking. Or maybe a rental car."

"If it goes sour, that's somebody else to identify you, Vince."

"Right you are."

"One rental sedan is enough."

"Any other improvements, Jerry?"

I went over it all in my mind. If Vince could get him into the car it all seemed clean enough. The hospital touch would make the courier's statement very damn confusing. And I felt better about not going back to the Tampa hotel. But I still didn't think much of the damn uniform.

"How about just a uniform cap, Vince? And I wear a gray suit. Then, at the hospital, I can leave the cap in the sedan. And, hell, you can wear it when you drive to the lot."

"I'd like to keep the complete uniform bit in."

"I wouldn't."

He grinned at me. "Okay. Just the uniform cap and you'll go ahead with it? Shake."

"Don't go so damn fast. How good is your information about the courier?"

"I got some of it from Carmela. I've made some contacts in that area, Jerry, and I checked it all out. The courier is scared witless about the whole thing. He spilled it all to his wife. They have two little girls. I'm convinced he's no problem."

"How about intercepting the money before he gets it?"

"Four of Melendez's agents escort him and it to the airplane."

"Suppose one goes along with him this time?"

"That would be a very sickening situation. Any one of the four would know me by sight. I think if I talked very, very fast I might turn it into a deal. But the odds are small, I mean that one would come along. And in that case, you're still in the clear. If there's a hassle, drive away from it. Ditch the car. Go home."

"Like you came into the water and hauled me out when I got shot in the shoulder?"

"Have I even hinted at that? Have I?"

"No."

"What's the word, Jerry?"

"When do you have to leave?"

"The ticket says one-fifteen tomorrow afternoon."

"Would you leave earlier or later if I said yes or no right now?"

"In any case, I'd have to grab the same airplane."

"So when you leave, you'll know."

"Will you give Lorraine the word?"

"If I say yes? Not a chance."

"Good. What will be the reason for your trip?"

"Job-hunting. Vince, if I say yes, I might need some financing. I'm that broke."

"No problem. I've got it with me."

"If I say yes."

"I heard you, boy. It has to be two. Just two. And I hope it's you. That's damn near a song lyric."

I started the car. "Copyright it, Uncle Vince. Make a mint."

"Somebody beat me to it. It had to be you. Remember?"

"Kindly don't sing it."

"One thing, Jerry. One last thing. Don't get futzed up with the morals of the thing. Peral is a tiger. Melendez is a shark. We are just a couple of cuties who zip in and grab the piece of meat and get out fast. And incidentally stop a nasty little civil war. Keep thinking of that. Hell, I hope you haven't gone too stale for the job, Jamison."

"Look, Vince. One thing. Just one guy in transit with all that money. Is that logical?"

"In the first place, Melendez has him thoroughly cowed. In the second place, it would attract attention to mount a guard on it. In the third place, he is put on at one end, watched at the stop en route, and picked up at this end, so where could he go, even if he got the yen?"

I drove back home. Lorraine had gone out some place, leaving no note or word with Irene. Irene fixed us lunch. We talked about old times and places. At one point I looked across the table at Vince and it struck me that I had never really known him, and never would. And I wondered if anybody had ever gotten close enough to him to be able to think they knew him well, how his mind and heart worked. He had the look of indolence and effectiveness of one of the great carnivores. There was a taint of the tiger in him. The tiger is not a herd beast.

I remembered a night long ago when we had flanked a patrol and sent them wildly down a slope to where our people had set the bamboo stakes at a fatal angle, cruelly barbed. The next day, at midmorning, Vince and I had gone back with some boys. There were still seven of them impaled on the stakes and four held to a thin thread of life. The rain came down. I remembered how Vince set the click of his grease gun to semi-automatic and sauntered down to where they were. I saw him in the haze of the rain curtain, on that morning when all the color had been leached out of the world, the broad brim of the Aussie hat protecting the smolder of the native cigar stub in the corner of his mouth. Like a man picking blooms in a strange garden, he had moved in that easy way from one to the other and shot each one in the head. The sound of the four shots went dead in the rain. Then he signaled and we came down and stripped them of weapons and ammunition and grenades and the contents of their pockets and any articles of clothing that might be useful to our people, and went back the way we had come.

And I remembered the way he liked to go off alone through the hills, and come back an hour or a day later. "Little friends, I have found a fine brisk little bridge with a permanent guard post." Then he would draw it up, sketching in the terrain and we would discuss ways and means.

All that life had become natural to me. But it was a long time back, and all this talk of planned revolution and millions and couriers seemed, in the quiet setting of my home, to be a rather extravagant and ambitious television spectacular which was falling flat.

But at times I could bring myself to believe it was all true. My tendency to believe, my ability to return to the thought and action patterns of twenty years ago was like a faulty fluorescent tube. It would glow steadily for a time, then falter and flicker.

I waited until I was driving him to the airport on Sunday. He hadn't pressed me for a decision. When I had to stop for a light I said, "Okay, Vince. We're back in business."

Though I heard no sound I had the impression he had exhaled in a long sigh. "Good deal, Jerry. Get to the Tampa Terrace before noon, or at least close to noon on the sixth. Make your own reservation. Pick a name. Something ordinary."

"Robert Martin."

"Okay. If there's any change there'll be a message at the desk for you. If not tell them it will be one or two nights and you'll let them know. Stay in the room and I'll get in touch. Better put the car in a lot somewhere near the hotel."

I let him off at the main entrance to the terminal. As we had approached he had taken five hundred in fifties from his wallet. I had protested, but he said if I didn't have to use it, I could give it back. He walked through the wide doors and out of sight, not looking back. On the way home I had to stop for another light. Two cops stood on the corner, talking. I looked at them and felt a barely perceptible quiver of uneasiness. I knew it was but the first of many symptoms.

On Sunday night a pack of Lorraine's special friends trooped in to drink my liquor. I had endured them for years, even tried to like them. Brittle, nervous, flirtatious women with laughter like the breaking of glass. And their dominated husbands, brown, drunk, noisy—masters of the crude double meaning, Don Juans of the locker room.

Now, by reason of the decision I had made, I was through with them. They were strangers.

That night before I went to bed I looked at myself in the bathroom mirror. And saw another stranger with a closed and wary face, coarse ginger hair going gray. I snapped the light out. The house was still. They had taken Lorraine off with them to the club, for drinking and groping and fumbling, for funny jokes and laughing, for wide slack kisses, and a fat tab added to the monthly statement.

I woke up when she came in. She turned all the bedroom lights on. I pretended sleep. I heard her leg thud into a chair, and heard her slurred and mumbled, "Son vabish." When she began to snore I got up and turned out the lights she had forgotten. In the darkness there was an odor of her in the room, stale perfume, smoke, liquor, and an acid trace of perspiration.

No place for Lorraine in my new world to be.

But room for Liz?

Chapter 4

I registered at the Tampa Terrace at ten minutes after noon on Tuesday, the sixth of May, as Robert Martin. I had my suit coat over my arm and my white shirt was pasted to my back from the exertion of walking the two and a half blocks from the parking lot. I was ninety per cent certain that there would be a note from Vince saying it was all off. But there was nothing at the desk for me.

After the bellhop closed the room door behind him, there was nothing to do but wait. I had left on Saturday morning, allowing three days for the sixteen-hundred-mile trip. I had hit a lot of heavy rains on the way down. Tampa was a blazing steam bath, but the room was air-conditioned.

I tried to read a magazine I had bought in the lobby, but I couldn't focus my mind on it. I walked back and forth, from the windows to the bureau, stubbing out cigarettes with only half an inch smoked from them. I cursed Vince for making me wait.

The twelve days in Vernon since Vince had left had been strange. Lorraine and her parents had the idea that I would get back to my meaningless job as soon as I "came to my senses." But I had gone back to the office only to pick up my final salary check. I had cashed it rather than deposit it. I had done some job-hunting, more as camouflage than anything else.

George Farr, one of the smartest and most successful builders in the entire area, surprised me by wanting to talk to me personally. I had expected the brush-off.

He leaned back and chewed on the bow of his glasses and said, "With all due respects to your father-in-law, Jerry, it's damn well time you cut yourself loose from that operation. Maybe it's a break for both of us. I need a top sergeant. The doc says I've got to shift to a lower gear. I need somebody to ramrod the jobs in progress, goose my supers, ride herd on materials, battle the architects, and asskiss the clients. I'll stay busy enough to feel important, but you'll be driven nuts. Three hundred fifty bucks a week and an annual bonus based on a percentage of the net. And you can start today."

It sounded good. It sounded damn good. And I could take Lorraine's offer. "It . . . it sounds fine. But I'll have to think it over."

"Right now we've got a shopping center, two motels, an automobile agency and a co-op apartment house on the

34

books. There's other stuff I want to bid on, but I haven't got the supervisory personnel."

"I'll have to let you know, George."

I felt dazed as I drove away. Dear Hotel—If anybody should try to leave a message for a fictitious Robert Martin, or ask for him at the desk on May sixth, kindly give him the enclosed envelope.

Dear Vince—Here is your five hundred. I am very sorry. I have decided I have no use for that much money after all. Thanks for yanking me out of the river that time.

When I went home Lorraine kept yapping at me. "What are you going to do? Just hang around the house? What are we going to live on?"

"I've got some plans."

"Fine. Great big brave plans. Mother was here while you were gone. She said Daddy's very upset about this whole thing. They can't understand why you've turned on him this way after all he's done. She cried, even."

"Lorraine. Get off my back."

"But what are you going to *do!*"

"I'm going to take a little trip."

"Where, for God's sake?"

"Look up some people I used to know. Maybe I'll be able to borrow enough money to get started on my own again."

"Who would lend *you* money?"

"They come running after me, trying to stuff it in my pocket. Why don't you go get a nice bottle and pass out some place?"

"It's my right to know what you're going to do!"

So I spent as little time as possible around the house. She was belting herself as never before. I learned how to make one beer in a neighborhood bar last a full hour.

On the Friday before I left I went, on impulse, to a drugstore near the office and phoned Liz and asked her if she could sneak out for coffee. She said she was caught up and E. J. was out and she'd be right along. She sat across from me in the booth and told me precisely how everything was going to hell. Even though I had left, I couldn't enjoy hearing that. You put a part of your life into something and it is a sad thing to hear how a stub-born and stupid old man is ruining it.

She seemed a little sad too. "Miss you around there, Jerry. I really do. It's dull around there. What are you going to do?"

I lied about job-hunting, about looking for backing.

"Hope you can start your own shop, Jerry. And I hope you'll need a gal in the office."

"Lorraine would just scream with joy if I hired you."

She looked at me steadily. "Would you care if she did?"

We were getting into places we had never been before. I looked back at her and said, "No. Maybe she's part of my past."

"What do you mean?"

"Suppose I've been lying, Liz. About job-hunting and setting up shop."

She frowned at me. "I don't follow you."

"I can't tell you much. I don't want to tell you much. Just suppose that I suddenly . . . came into a large chunk of money. Large."

"How nice for you."

"I'm going away for a while. I may come back with it."

There was sudden comprehension and concern. "You wouldn't do anything . . . really stupid?"

"No. It would be safe. Money to keep."

Her hand rested beside her coffee cup. I reached across the booth and took hold of her hand and wrist. I saw from the way the shape of her mouth changed that I had gripped her too tightly and hurt her. She made no protest. I had not touched her before.

"Maybe when I come back with it, we could take off for good."

"Where?"

"There'd be enough to go anywhere."

She looked beyond me, her stare curiously intent. She ran the tip of her tongue across her lower lip. "It's a dull life here, Jerry. It's getting duller instead of better."

"Later we could make it legal."

"Later we can talk about it. We can talk about the whole thing. Just get the money."

I released her hand. She sipped her coffee. She looked at me over the rim of the cup. She set it down empty and gave me a wry smile of guilt and promise that quickened my heart. "Get the money," she said in almost a whisper. "Then we'll talk."

I left on Saturday after a messy brawl with Lorraine. I had a little over a thousand dollars with me. I drove southeast through heavy rains. Mr. Robert Martin, lying on sagging beds, watching on old ceilings the light patterns of the traffic and the colored neon, smelling the effluvium of questionable plumbing and the rankness of old linoleum, hearing in the trafficky night the empty bam of a juke box base, a girl-laugh like a shriek of anguish, and beyond the thin wall, the dreary honking of a phlegm-ridden salesman of plastic novelties.

The room phone rang at twenty past three. I answered it and Vince said he'd be right up. He came in striding lithely, taut, brown and grinning. He wore a cocoa straw hat, massive sun glasses. As I closed the door he tossed a brown paper bag on the bed. He went over to the bureau and looked at the brimming ash tray.

"We're a little jumpy today, aren't we?"

"Cut it out, damn it!"

He went over and opened the bag and flipped the chauffeur hat to me. I put it on. It was a half size small, but I could pull it down so that it looked right.

"Where's the gray suit?" I opened the closet door. He looked at it. "Okay. We'll pick up a black bow tie. It'll look more like a uniform then."

He took his hat and glasses off and lay on the bed. "Our little man comes in tomorrow on 675 at three in the afternoon."

"Nothing has changed? Nothing has gone sour?"

"You keep this up and you could hurt my feelings. I have a rental sedan. Raoul thinks I'm in São Paulo taking care of a little matter for him. Carmela is all alerted.

37

General Peral will receive the detailed account of vile conspiracy at three tomorrow his time. Four o'clock here. It's all a big delicious piece of cake, Jerry boy, oozing chocolate."

"So what now?"

He swung off the bed and went to the bureau and took a city map out of his pocket. The route was marked. I studied it. We went down to the street. The sedan was in a metered parking slot. It was a black Chrysler, about three years old, and highly polished. We went out to Tampa International, slowed by the curbing in front of the main doors, then turned out again. He held the map and the watch, and told me what speed to maintain in each portion of the trip. It was an involved route, ending at the hospital. We went back and went over it again, and I made two small errors. When I did it the third time, I was perfect. Then we started from where my car would be parked, and found the quickest possible way to the department store and from there to Route 301 north. It was not sufficiently complicated to require going over a second time.

When it was time for evening visiting hours at the hospital, we went in through the side door where I would be leaving, and found our way to the corridor to the emergency ward. Vince had made one small change in plans. He had been able to rent the sedan at a centrally located place. He said it seemed smart, and I agreed, to return the sedan and pay the rental fee. He had acquired a small bottle of gasoline and it would take but a moment to wipe the decal off the sedan door. He would put the decal on as near to the time of arrival of the flight as seemed feasible.

We parted near the hotel at ten o'clock on Tuesday night. He said he had a place to stay. I slept poorly. In the morning I dressed in white shirt, black bow tie, gray suit. I had coffee in the hotel and then checked out and carried my suitcase and the hat in the paper bag to my car, put the suitcase in and relocked it. I had but a three-minute wait out in front of the parking lot before Vince came along in the black Chrysler. I put the bag on the floor in back and took the wheel. We made a final run-through, paying particular attention to time. Twenty-eight minutes, plus or minus two minutes depending on traffic and lights from Tampa International to the hospital. Three minutes after arrival, I would be in my car with the money. Vince had to dispose of the pouch and the hat, return the sedan, remove the decal, and walk six blocks. We allowed thirty minutes for that. It would take me only ten minutes to drive to the department store. That would leave me twenty minutes dead time. It was decided I would cruise around the block for twenty minutes. He would spot the car and I would pick him up on the fly. It added up to seventy-three minutes. If the flight was on time, we should be out of town and headed north by quarter after four.

Vince had his own suitcase in the Chrysler. We had sandwiches and coffee at twelve-thirty. The rehearsals had given me a feeling of confidence. I knew that I could do precisely what was expected of me. Vince had found the mailbox where he would dispose of the pouch and the trash container where he would leave the hat. We drove to the lot. I drove my car, with him following me, and we parked mine across from the side entrance of the hospital. We transferred his suitcase to my car and re-locked it. It was a quiet street. He moistened the stolen decal, slid it deftly off its backing onto the sheen of the black door. I put on the chauffeur hat. He sat in the back of the Chrysler. We drove toward the airport and parked a few minutes away from the main entrance. He took out the hypo case and loaded the cylinder, sucking the demerol up through the rubber top of the small bottle, and wedged the hypo down behind the seat on the side where he would sit.

"You know the right dosage?"

"To the last cc. They'll get him awake no earlier than seven tonight. And Señor Zaragosa has damn little English, and by then the consulate will be closed and they will have met the wrong plane and it'll all be one big confusion."

"Now it all depends on your getting him into the car."

"I'll get him into the car, sweetheart."

"I don't really believe in the money yet. Not that much money."

"Wait until you start fondling it." He looked at his watch. "About another six minutes until kickoff."

It was a busy airport. They were coming in and taking off. The parked car was an oven. I was sweating through my suit. The tight hat was giving me a headache.

"Let's roll it," Vince said.

I drove to the airport and turned in the main drive. I passed the entrance to the parking lot and swung around and parked where we had planned, just to the left of the main doors for anyone coming out. It was ten minutes of three. Vince got out. A guard came over and said, "Buddy, you can't park in here."

Vince gave him a broad grin, a half bow, and a flood of Spanish.

"I don't know what you're saying but you can't leave it here."

Vince, still beaming, patted the black fender and said, *"Diplomático! Diplomático! Offeeessssial!"*

Another guard came over and said, "It's okay, Harry. It's okay for them jokers to park it in front." They went away.

Vince went in. He was gone five minutes. He came out alone and came to my window and said, "Be of good cheer, baby. I just made a phone call. Señor Zaragosa is expected at eight-fifteen this evening."

It felt very comforting to be able to stop watching for the legitimate sedan. "Is the flight on time?"

"On the button." He straightened up and looked toward the southwest. "And that very well could be it." He punched my shoulder hard. The white teeth gleamed quickly. He went back inside.

The minutes went by. I watched the main doors. I'd had the same feeling before when, once the ambush had been carefully arranged, all you had to do was wait for the far-off sound of truck engines. Or for the first sight of a platoon on the trail. Then you'd let their point go by and hope to hell he didn't spot anything. And when the last

40

man was within the ambush zone, Vince would open up and the first violent hammering of the weapon on full automatic would be lost in the surging chattering crash as we opened up with all we had. . . .

Vince came out through the main doors. There was a stocky man with him, a man in a dark suit and a white straw hat, a man with a pale pyramidal face, heavy jowls dark with beard shadow, a pursed red mouth and sunken eyes. The small man carried a diplomatic pouch and a briefcase. Vince carried a large black suitcase as though it were very heavy. It was of black shiny metal with chrome corners and hardware. The chrome was dull and corroded, and there were dents in the black metal. Vince was talking volubly, gesturing with his free hand. The man had a remote and troubled look and his steps were lagging. Vince seemed to be urging him along.

I got out, as instructed, and went around the rear of the car and opened the rear door, then went ahead and took the suitcase from Vince. I grunted when the strain came on my arm. It was like lead.

The little man said sharply to me, *"Momento! Alto!"*

I paid no attention. I opened the front door and heaved the suitcase on to the front seat. I slammed the door. Vince had the man by the arm, urging him toward the car. The man seemed to shrug and came toward the car. It was going to be all right. It was going to work.

But then I saw the two men coming rapidly toward them, coming up behind them. Two lean men in sports shirts and pale jackets, focused on Vince and Zaragosa with an unmistakable intensity. And one hand coming out of the side pocket of a vivid yellow jacket, bringing with it a blued gleam of metal that was incongruous in the bright hot sunlight.

"Behind you!" I yelled.

As Vince spun around a slug at a range of ten feet knocked him a half step off balance. With perfect instinct and his miraculous reflexes, he swung Zaragosa in front of him and, in the same instant said, "Get the wheel!"

41

I ran around the rear of the car. I skidded on the paving. I felt as if I were running in a dream, trying to run through waist-deep water. I heard two more shots. I could hear some people yelling, hear running footsteps, hear a woman's startled scream. I piled into the car and turned the key and the motor caught.

The two men were close. I saw Vince, with horrid effort, swing the dumpy weight of Zaragosa by crotch and neck and hurl him at the two men. It tumbled one of them and the other made a wild leap to jump clear, but landed off balance and fell. As Vince fell into the back I stepped the gas to the floor and swung in a wide screaming arc and aimed for the entrance from the highway. A fat man leaped, roaring, for his life. A guard jumped out, waving his arms, and jumped back. I heard Vince yank the back door shut. I took one quick glance in the rear-vision mirror. Both men were running hard. Zaragosa was on the sidewalk, his briefcase and the diplomatic pouch ten feet from him.

I picked a small hole in traffic and barreled out without stopping, wedging it larger as brakes yelped behind me and angry horns blew. When I came to the right turn toward town I was doing eighty. I hit the brake and slid through the turn and yanked it straight. I thought I heard a far-off siren. I passed other cars fast and wide, forcing oncoming traffic way over. I banged the brakes again, cut hard behind an oncoming truck into the left turn on the route we had practiced. I slowed to proper sedateness and, three blocks later, a light stopped us.

Vince was on the floor in back. "How bad?" I asked him.

"I don't know. I'm bleeding like a pig."

"Can you do anything about it?"

"I'm trying to do something about it. Jesus!"

"How about what's his name?" I asked, starting up as the light changed.

"When he took the second one I felt all the bones go out of him. I think he had it good."

"Who the hell were they?"

"I think I've seen one of them before, but I don't know

42

where. So they wouldn't be Kyodos's people. Some kind of a leak, I think. Somebody with the same idea. Son of a bitch." There was a wince of pain in his voice.

"Where are you hit?"

"High on the right, just over the collarbone. That was the first one. And the left thigh, high and inside."

"Could you drive a car?"

"Christ, no! I'm beginning to feel a little foggy already." I remembered the chauffeur hat and dropped it on the floor beside me.

"Want to risk the hospital?"

"That would be the end, wouldn't it, sweetheart? Let's go where we can get this leaking stopped. And in a hurry."

I drove as fast as I dared, circled the hospital and was able to park directly behind my station wagon. There was not much traffic on the street. I moved the black tin suitcase into the back end of the wagon. I went back to the Chrysler. One rear window was starred by a slug. I opened the door a crack.

"Can you make it to the wagon?"

"I've got to make it to the wagon," he said. He had a soapy look under his tan. There was a sweet spoiled smell of blood in the car. Fortunately his suit was dark. The left pant leg was heavy with blood, as was the right side of his chest and the right side of his back. I helped him onto his feet and tried to get him to lean on me, but he straightened himself and walked slowly and steadily to the station wagon and got in. He closed his eyes, fumbled in a pocket, brought out a handkerchief and a small bottle of clear fluid.

"Might as well do all we can," he said. His voice was weak. "Hypo, decal, fingerprints."

I worked as quickly and thoroughly as I could. A small boy stood on the sidewalk and watched me solemnly. I left the keys in the ignition in the hope the car would be stolen.

"That looks like a bullet did it," the small boy said, staring at the rear window.

"No. A kid did it with a rock. He looked just like you." He thought that over and went away. I dropped the bot-

43

tle of gas in the gutter. I took the chauffeur hat and walked to the wagon and started it up and headed north toward Route 92.

"How are you holding up?"

He was slouched in the seat, eyes closed. "Don't waste too much time."

When I turned off 92 onto 301 we were soon in empty country. I looked at my watch. Almost four. And Vince had been bleeding since about ten after three. He looked bad. I turned on an obscure road, turned off it onto a dirt road and pulled off in a small hollow between two knolls. I parked in such a way that the bulk of the car would hide him from anybody who might come down the road. He was able to get out by himself. He stretched out on the ground. I pulled the trousers off. I knew I would find no spurting of bright arterial blood. Had that been the case he wouldn't have lived until we got to the hospital. Venous blood came darkly, slowly, steadily from a round hole punched in the inside meat of his left thigh and from a larger ragged hole in the rear of the thigh. I opened my suitcase, ripped up a white shirt, made a pad for front and rear wound. I had two thirds of a pint of bourbon, souvenir of a dreary motel night in Tennessee. I splashed bourbon onto the torn flesh and onto the shirt sleeves.

"I smell a heavenly fragrance," he said.

"Shut up. Sit up so I can get your shirt off."

The shoulder wound was not bleeding as badly, but it had an uglier look. I think the slug nicked the collarbone so that when it emerged it was tumbling. The thick shoulder muscles looked badly ripped. I used the same treatment, and rigged a sling for his right arm out of two halves of a shirt sleeve after I helped him into a fresh shirt from his suitcase. I got him into dark blue slacks. I scraped a hole with the tire iron and buried the ruined suit and shirt. After he had taken the second long drink from the bourbon bottle, his color improved.

"Thank you, Doctor Jamison," he said.

"You're going to need a legitimate doctor."

"In good time."

44

"What the hell do we do now, Vince?"

"Hole up where we can look at the money."

I helped him into the car. I drove back to Route 301. I thought we should stop as soon as we found a place, but he wanted to put more miles between us and Tampa. I remembered the chauffeur's hat and scaled it out into some heavy roadside scrub.

I picked up the five o'clock news out of a Tampa station on the car radio. He covered the international and national scene in about twelve seconds and then got down to the meat. He seemed to be getting a big boot out of it. It must have been a dull week in Tampa until all this happened.

Señor Alvaro Zaragosa was entirely dead, mostly of a bullet through the heart. The killers had attacked the "diplomat" from ———— while he was standing talking to an unknown man beside a chauffeur-driven sedan in front of the terminal building at Tampa International Airport. The unknown man had made good his escape in the sedan in a "hail of bullets." The assassins had escaped in a blue and white Ford sedan bearing local license plates. The "diplomat" had arrived from South America on a three o'clock flight en route to the regional consular office in Tampa. The diplomatic pouch and other official papers were left behind by the assassins when they fled. The man attacked along with the dead "diplomat" was described as tall, swarthy, powerfully built, wearing a dark brown suit, a straw hat and sun glasses. It was believed that he spoke no English. The consul, when contacted, had no comment to make on the assassination. Police had blocked all roads and were still looking for the chauffeur-driven sedan and the blue and white Ford. He gave a very sketchy and somewhat erroneous description of the gunmen.

When he started on the baseball scores, I turned it off.

"We got through before the road-blocking bit," Vince said.

"It looks that way."

"I'll bet that consul is very damned confused. People

will come winging down from Washington. But there shouldn't be any big hooraw about it."

"No?"

"Why should there be? Zaragosa was a nonentity. Nothing is missing. They'll figure that the little man had gotten himself mixed up in some kind of a smuggling deal, and it was a falling out of thieves. And they won't want to have an abuse of diplomatic courtesy publicized. Kyodos may be mildly disappointed but he won't give too much of a damn. There's always a market for his products. And he'll tie it up with Peral smashing Melendez. I'm surprised it wasn't on the news wires in time for that joker to let us know about it. It might come out just fine, Jerry."

"Sure. It's fine. You've got two bad holes in your hide, one man is dead, and those two playmates are undoubtedly looking for us. Everything looks rosy."

"Pile on some more miles, Jerry boy. Move this wagon."

At the time of the six o'clock news we were just beyond Ocala. I missed the hour by a few moments and turned on the radio in the middle of one of those self-nominated oracles with a voice like a mixture of corn syrup and cathedral bells: ". . . little news out of the country, we do know that the strong man, General Peral, with the loyal assistance of his small but effective professional army, has utterly crushed the Melendez revolt. The capital city is under martial law this evening, and all citizens have been requested to stay off the streets. Reliable sources have informed your reporter that except for the few who were shot down resisting arrest, the entire Melendez group has been captured and imprisoned. The insurgent strong point at Melendez's Hacienda de las Tres Marias has not yet been reduced, but it is completely surrounded and surrender is expected momentarily, if indeed it has not already occurred.

"Your reporter has warned many times of the danger to the free world of such revolts. This would appear to be another Communist-inspired attempt to upset the government of one of the strong friends of this country. It appears that the Melendez group has been stockpiling

46

weapons for many months, and it was only through chance, through some circumstance we will never know, that the government was advised in time."

"How wrong can you be?" Vince said.

"We have just received a new bulletin, and it seems to add the final touch to our story. Raoul Melendez employed a beautiful personal secretary named Carmela de la Vega. In some way Carmela received warning in advance of the government's move to crush the incipient rebellion. Though not a licensed pilot she took off today in a single-engine airplane owned by Melendez in a desperate attempt to cross the border and land, two hundred miles away, at the city of Viadiad. It is perhaps possible that as a loyal citizen of the Americas, she was the one who informed Peral, then fled in case the Melendez forces should achieve victory and control. Perhaps she planned to land and disappear. We shall never know. For Carmela de la Vega's desperate gamble did not pay off. She crashed on landing and was instantly killed."

A younger sounding man with an even more unctuous and juicy voice began to advertise a dainty deodorant. I turned it off. I took my eyes from the traffic to glance at Vince. His face was carved from hard stained wood. There was no expression on it.

"Flew it right into the ground," he said finally. "Had the tendency. Lousy depth perception. Either bang it in hard, or try to land thirty feet in the air."

"How much farther can you go?" I asked him.

"Not too far, Jerry. I lost too damn much fluid. I've got to have water pretty soon."

We holed up at Stark, Florida. The motel was new. It was after dark. The round and pleasant woman behind the desk told me that she had a twin bed double. I said I would sign for my friend if it was all right. He was asleep when I pulled in, I told her. She said that would be fine. The boy would show us where to park and bring ice.

I followed the boy and parked by Number 20. After he had unlocked it and handed me the key, I sent him after ice. While he was gone I helped Vince inside. He could barely walk even leaning most of his weight on me. I

47

met the boy at the door when he brought the ice, and tipped him. I brought the luggage in, made certain the door was locked. I fixed the blinds and pulled the draperies across the windows. The air-conditioner huffed and whined busily. Vince sat in the only armchair. It took five glasses of water before he felt satisfied.

"Better get to bed."

"First I look at what we've got. First I want to be sure we haven't got a suitcase full of roof tiles, baby."

"That's a hell of a thought."

I put the suitcase on the floor in front of the chair, on its side. It was locked. The two locks were sturdy. I went out and got the tire iron. I pried the locks open, opened the suitcase. A piece of coarse off-white cloth covered the contents. I snatched it off and looked at what we had.

Chapter 5

A one-dollar bill has a humble and homely look. A five-dollar bill has a few meek pretensions. A ten is vigorous and forthright and honest, like a scout leader. A twenty, held to the ear like a seashell, emits the far-off sound of nightclub music. A fifty wears the faint sneer of race track. It has a portly look, needs a shave, wears a yellow diamond on the little finger. And a hundred is very haughty indeed.

Then there is quantity. A wad of ones in the bottom of a grubby pocket, or fanned between the fingers in an alley game. Or three frayed fives in a flat cheap billfold. Then there is the flashy billfold, padded fat with ones and fives and tens and twenties. Next step is the platinum bill clip, with its dainty burden of twenties and fifties, crisp and folded but once. After that is the unmarked envelope with its cool sheaf of hundreds, slipped from hand to hand in the corridor of a government building.

Or there are banks. And when you get up to the window there is a stack at the teller's elbow that can stop your heart.

When cute little girls visit the mint the kind man sometimes lets them hold a million dollars. In ten-thousand-dollar bills, the sort of bills that circulate inside the mysterious and cabalistic recesses of the Federal Exchange System. One hundred of them. A little packet only so thick for a whole million dollars. And if the little girl should cut and run with it, it wouldn't do her a damn bit of good.

But there was nothing like what I looked at when I whipped that piece of cloth aside. Nothing. I was one man when I pried the locks loose. And I was somebody else after I looked at the money. And I knew in some crazy way that I couldn't ever go back to being the man who pried the locks, no matter how desperately I might want to.

I was sitting on my heels. I looked up at Vince in the chair. Our eyes met, and we looked at each other in a strange way for a moment or two, with shame and guilt and a high, wild, uncomfortable exaltation. And looked away in awkwardness.

"At a time like this," Vince said, "what does one say?"

"One says count it."

The bills were wired together in bricks about four inches thick, two strands of wire around each brick twisted tightly about one inch from the end of each brick, and cut off. The bricks were tightly fitted into the suitcase. I pulled one out. The top and bottom bill were both hundreds. Neither was new. I bounced it in my palm and frowned at it. Vince asked to see it and I handed it to him. He held it between his knees and riffled the tightly packed edges of the bills with the thumb of his left hand.

"Probably five hundred of them," he said.

"Fifty thousand in a block."

"So how many blocks?"

I pulled them out, counting them as I pulled them out. It seemed to be a thing you should do slowly, but my eye kept racing ahead. Sixty-eight blocks of hundreds.

And one block of five-hundred-dollar bills, the same size.

"I can't do it in my head," Vince said breathlessly. "Jerry, that block of five hundreds. That's a quarter of a million bucks. Get a pencil and paper and we'll—"

"Hold it." I took the scrap of paper out of the bottom. It had been hidden by the money. Figures typed on an ancient machine with a worn-out ribbon, type badly out of alignment. I looked at it and handed it to him.

$$34,000 \times \$100 = \$3,400,000$$
$$500 \times \$500 = \underline{250,000}$$
$$\$3,650,000$$

I got a pencil and paper from the desk. Sixty-eight times five hundred made thirty-four thousand, so there were five hundred in a brick. I wouldn't have expected there to be thirty-four thousand hundred-dollar bills in existence. Two million for Vince and one for me.

"Carmela is out?" I said.

"You heard the man. So everything over three is down the middle."

So I had one million three hundred and twenty-five thousand bucks all my own. I looked at the stacked money. "We'll have to bust a brick."

"Go ahead."

The wire was too heavy to untwist. I used the tire iron. I tore the top bill badly. When the wire popped, the bills took up a hell of a lot more room. I reassembled the toppled stack and cut the deck in half by eye. I counted one half. Two hundred and sixty-two of them. So I took twelve off and put it with the other stack. I took my two hundred and fifty bills over and put them in my suitcase, under my underwear. Small change. Twenty-five thousand lousy bucks. The torn one was on top. I waved it at Vince. "Better throw this one away."

"Hell no. Give it here and take one of mine."

"Can you spare it?"

"For a friend."

I got out the cigarettes and lighter. He held the torn

bill. I lit it. He held it out and lit my cigarette and then lit his own. He held it by the corner until it burned down to his fingers.

"Never thought I'd get to do that," he said.

And suddenly we were laughing in a gasping, gone way as if we were hopped up or had lost our minds. Then I remembered his five hundred and wanted to return that to him, but he said no, I was insulting him. We divided the big pile. I came out with twenty-six bricks of hundreds. He said he would take the five hundreds. Where he would be, he said, he could unload them easier.

I looked at my stack and arranged it in a new way. I looked at his stack of money. And felt a sudden twinge of resentment. His was a fatter, more florid, more overwhelming pile. Then told myself I was being a child. Once we knew the split, I packed it all back in the tin suitcase. Though the locks were gone, I had pried so carefully they would latch and keep the bag shut. I put it in the big closet and shut the door. I brought him more water, then helped him into the bathroom, then helped him undress and get into bed. He said he had begun to stiffen up. I knew the feeling.

I went out and drove around and found a diner and ate and brought him back two hamburgers and a container of coffee. When I unlocked the door I had the ridiculous hunch, but absurdly strong, that he and the money would be gone.

But he was asleep. I thought he should eat so I woke him up. He managed one hamburger and half the coffee.

"Now what?" I said.

"Now we see how I mend."

"It isn't going to be very fast."

"If the meat doesn't start to spoil, ten days should do it. Then I can be on my way."

"Where?"

"I've got a spot and a way to get there. And Carmela's little booboo means I don't have to make a side trip."

"What I don't know won't hurt you?"

"Precisely."

"So for the ten days?"

"The safest and most comfortable place I can think of, Jerry, is your house."

I thought that over. He was right, but it was an imposition. I wanted to be rid of him. He could be tied to the mess a lot more readily than I could.

"Look, did you enter legally?"

"This time, yes."

"But I take you home and it increases my risk."

"That's a fair statement."

"The more the risk, the more the profit, Vince."

He looked at me for long seconds, then yawned and said, "Name it."

"One more stack of the little ones."

"That's a hell of a high rate. That's a hell of a rental."

I do not think the man who pried the suitcase open would have tried to make that kind of a deal. But I wasn't that man. I wasn't as soft as he was.

"The alternative, Vince, is I find you a place to stay. I'll look in on you once a day and bring food."

"What will that cost me?"

"There's no charge."

He shut his eyes. Just when I thought he had fallen asleep he opened them. "Okay. Your house. Now you've got twenty-seven toys to play with. Maybe you can gouge a few more out of me."

"Kindly go to hell, Biskay. It's no skin off you anyway. Five of your bundles of little ones would have gone to Carmela. So you're still four bundles ahead. And, my friend, I could have swung that car out of there while you were playing volleyball with Zaragosa."

He shut his eyes again and said, "Good night, dear old pal. That's why I picked you, remember? Because you wouldn't drive away."

The next day he was in agony whenever he tried to move. We didn't get on the road until a little after ten. He slept frequently, and groaned aloud in his sleep. When I found a drive-in for lunch he couldn't eat. When I looked at him in the late afternoon his eyes had an odd look. I put the back of my hand against his forehead.

"Fever?" he asked.

"Man, you feel like a stove."

"It's the leg."

"We've got to find a doctor."

"Hell with it. I'm tough. Keep rolling, lieutenant."

But an hour later, just outside of Birmingham, he started spouting off in Spanish, and he tried to open the door at sixty-five. I yanked him back. He went quickly into a stupor, mumbling constantly.

I signed us into a motel the other side of Birmingham, on 78 to Memphis, and had a hell of a job getting him into the room. I got a unit way in the back. He was out. I thought of how easy it would be to just walk out with the money. All of it. Just idle speculation.

I took enough money with me and went back to Birmingham and found a cheap doctor on a cheap street who thought five thousand in hundreds was all the money in the world. Enough to warrant not reporting the wounds of a man who had accidentally shot himself. Twice. I brought him back to the motel and he dispensed shots and pills and dressed the wounds, and I took him back where I got him. He said Vince shouldn't travel for a few days.

I was up at dawn. Vince was weak and lucid. His eyes looked sunken. I explained about the doctor and what he had said. Vince said that if I could get him into the car, he could ride in it. I borrowed four blankets from the motel to make a bed in the rear of the wagon, and left a fifty-dollar bill in an envelope for the manager, just in case he had corrected the license number I had written down.

Vince had a hell of a day. The pain of travel turned him a yellow-gray. After dark I parked beside the road and slept for two hours. Then I went on through the night, through Springfield and Preston and Kansas City, pushing the car. We got home at five o'clock on Saturday afternoon, road-raveled and exhausted. I hoped Lorraine wasn't home. She wasn't. Nor was Irene. I got

53

him in and up the stairs. He couldn't walk up. I didn't want to risk a fall. He sat on each stair and helped as much as he could when I hoisted him up to the next one. He'd lost a lot of weight fast, but he was still too damn big to carry.

I got him undressed and into a pair of pajamas and into the guest-room bed where he had stayed such a short time before.

The total job took forty minutes. Then I faced the problem of the money. Lorraine had too active and inquisitive a mind. And I knew she'd be prying to find out where I'd been and what I'd been doing. I horsed the black suitcase down the cellar stairs. The house had oil heat but it had originally been designed for coal with an automatic stoker. I kept the hardwood for the fireplace in the bin. They could load it directly into the basement from the truck and then stack it. There was a lot of it—oak, birch and maple—nearly two cords, all stacked. I figured that damn suitcase weighed better than a hundred pounds, and the poorly designed handle cut and pinched your hand. I put on the bin light, laid the suitcase flat and restacked the wood over it, working so fast I drove splinters into my hands. We hadn't used the fireplace much the previous winter. Fireplaces go with long contented evenings of marriage. We had come to the point where we had a fire only when we had a party.

There were enough short chunks so I could do a fair job. I went back and washed my hands and dug out the more obvious splinters with Lorraine's eyebrow tweezers. I wanted a shower badly, but there was still the problem of the twenty-five thousand in my suitcase. I transferred five hundred to my wallet, put the rest in a heavy manila envelope, took the bottom drawer of my bureau all the way out and fastened the envelope to the back of it with masking tape. It was bulky enough to keep the drawer from shutting all the way, but I judged it safe enough.

It was after six. I went in to check on Vince. He was sleeping lightly. I sat on the edge of the bed and he woke up.

"How are you doing?"

"My God, I'm glad to get off that highway. Hell is a place where they keep you in a station wagon."

"We haven't had much chance to talk. I've got to tell Lorraine something."

"Don't tell her much."

"Making a big mystery out of it is just as bad."

"I see what you mean, Jerry."

"It would be nice to leave bullets out of it. Give her the idea of bullets and she'll take off from there. Three drinks and she'll make a big deal out of it. It's got to be something dull."

"There isn't a duller damn thing in the world, Jerry, than somebody else's operation."

"Good idea, but what kind?"

"Make it a bursitis sort of thing. They opened up my shoulder and my hip and scraped guck off the bone or whatever the hell you do."

"Okay. You told me when you were here before that you were going to have the operation. You can say you told Lorraine too. She hears so much when she's swacked that she doesn't remember that she'll go along with that. So I stopped in to see how you were doing. But where?"

"Make it Philadelphia."

It sounded all right. I'd brought Vince back home. Lorraine wouldn't object, not about Vince. Not with the way she reacted to him.

"How about the money?" he asked.

"It's safe."

He looked at me. "That's nice. That's a good thing to know. But where is it?"

"I told you it's safe."

He rolled up onto his left elbow with an effort. The low sun came through the west windows. The beard stubble was touched by the sun, dark, yet with a look of copper.

"Jerry, let's try to keep this thing under control. It's a lot of money. It is so damn much money that it can distort you, bitch up the way you think when you're standing too close to it. I think I should know where it is."

"In the cellar. In the coal bin. I stacked cordwood over it."

He sighed as he lay back. "That's just fine," he said.

And I heard the brisk and busy chugging of Lorraine's Porsche as she swung into the drive.

I went downstairs, met her as she came into the kitchen. "Well, hello indeed," she said. She wore a brief gay swimsuit, a hip-length blue terry beach coat. Dampness had coiled her dark hair tightly.

"Swimming?"

She took an ice tray over to the counter. "Heavens, no! I've been tea dancing. Did you have a nice little trip, dahling?"

"It was all right. I brought back a house guest."

She dropped ice in her glass and whirled and glared at me. "What kind of a ridiculous . . ."

"You remember Vince telling us about the operation he had to have. That bone thing on his shoulder and his hip."

Her eyes clouded. She bit her underlip. "Sort of vaguely, I guess."

"I dropped in on him in Philadelphia to see how he was doing."

"You went all the way to Philadelphia!"

"I've been a lot of places. He wasn't set up too well there. So I talked him into coming back with me. He'll have to stay in bed a while."

"The poor lamb!"

"You don't mind?"

"Goodness! I don't mind. Irene might. But she certainly hasn't had much to do around here lately. Gosh, I told her she could go after lunch. What about food for Vince?"

"He won't want much. Soup and toast. I can eat out."

"I'm having dinner at the club. I can fix him something before I go." She looked at me closely. "Jerry, you look like hell. You look haggard."

"I did a lot of driving."

She carried her full drink upstairs. When I went to

our room I heard her talking to Vince, heard his deep voice as he answered her.

I took a fast shower. When I went into the bedroom in my shorts Lorraine stood in her robe by my bureau looking at a folder of paper matches.

"You certainly did get around, darling. These matches are from a motel in Stark, Florida."

"I . . . I didn't get that far. I must have picked them up in another motel. Maybe it's a chain."

"The checking account is down to practically nothing. What are you going to do about it?"

"I'll put some in. But not much. Lorraine, you've got to take it easy. Things aren't the way they used to be."

"Whose fault is that? You could start again with Daddy on Monday, couldn't you?"

"Just take it easy, will you?"

"Maybe I will and maybe I won't. What are you going to do about a job?"

"I haven't decided."

"So your dear dear friends wouldn't loan you a dime. I'm not surprised. You'd better decide what you're going to do. People are going to think you're a little touched. Doesn't Vince look horrible?"

"I guess he was pretty sick."

"I don't think he was in any shape to ride so far."

"He's tough."

After she showered she fixed soup and toast for Vince. Then she changed from her robe to a cocktail dress. I stood at Vince's window and watched her drive away, the top down on the little car, her black hair tied in place with a colorful kerchief. I heard the rattle as Vince set his tray aside.

I helped him to the bathroom, and then got him settled for the night, water, pills and alarm clock on the night stand. I felt that there was something we should talk over, but my mind was too dulled by fatigue. I was too damn tired to eat out. I put Vince's tray in the kitchen. I ate the piece of toast he had left, drank most of a quart of milk and went to bed, and sleep came so fast it was like drowning in a pool of warm black ink.

Chapter 6

When I woke up at ten Lorraine was still asleep. Irene had Sundays off. I went down and got the Sunday paper out of the hedge where the carrier had thrown it, put coffee on, and went through the paper carefully.

There was a long and leisurely analysis of the Melendez revolt. Señor Raoul Melendez had unfortunately hung himself in his cell in the federal prison in the capital. The rebellion was completely crushed, and the stockpiled arms had been taken over by General Peral's army. All key figures in the revolt were either dead or under arrest. Melendez's extensive holdings had been taken over by the Minister of the Interior. The curfew had been lifted, and it was believed there would be no adverse effect on the tourist industry.

Near the bottom of the long article was one significant little paragraph. It followed the account of Carmela de la Vega's unfortunate flight.

> Also being sought is Melendez's personal pilot and confidential aide, an American-born naturalized citizen of the country named Vincente Biskay. It has been established that Biskay left the country by commercial air transport on May fourth, four days before the rebellion. His destination is not known. In view of his close association with Melendez over a period of years, it is not considered likely that he will return. Informed sources believe that Biskay may seek political asylum in Cuba where the Melendez family retains extensive interests. Biskay was regarded as a man of mystery and a soldier of fortune.

The murder in Tampa was also given considerable coverage, but nowhere in either news report was there any hint of any connection between the two happenings. The blue and white Ford had been recovered in Ybor City, the Latin section of Tampa, and it was established that it had been stolen from a parking lot in downtown Tampa at about one o'clock, two hours before the shooting. The black chauffeur-driven sedan in which the swarthy stranger had escaped the killers had been located by Tampa police and proved to be a rental sedan. According to the rental agency records, the man who had rented it was a local resident named Daniel Harland, a commercial fisherman. When Harland was picked up and questioned by the police he told of being stopped on the street by a well-dressed man who asked Harland if he had a driver's license and had it with him. Harland said he did. When Harland agreed to help the man, they walked to within half a block of the rental agency. The stranger sent Harland in with a one-hundred-dollar deposit and instructions to rent a black sedan in the medium- to high-price range. When Harland turned the car over to the stranger, the man gave him the fifty dollars he had promised him for his trouble.

When the car was recovered one window had been shattered by a bullet, and there was a considerable quantity of blood on the floor in the back, leading the police to believe that the man who escaped the killers had been seriously wounded. All area doctors had been warned to be on the alert for anyone requiring treatment of a bullet wound.

The police had found smudged and indistinct fingerprints on both vehicles, and it was not yet known if they could be used for identification purposes.

The Ambassador from ——— in Washington had made a low-key and cautious statement to the effect that no official papers were missing, that the crime was apparently without political motivation, and it was probable that there had been some personal reason for the murder of Señor Alvaro Zaragosa.

When I took the paper and some coffee up to Vince, he was in the bathroom. When he came out I hurried to help him. He was chalky under his tan, lips tightly compressed, eyes squeezed by pain. I helped him to the bed. He stretched out and slowly his color improved.

"Why didn't you holler?"

"Got to get the machine running sometime. Stood up too damn long shaving. Came close to passing out." He propped himself up on the pillows and I handed him his coffee.

"Are we in the headlines?" he asked, noticing the newspaper.

"You're mentioned by name."

He seemed to stop breathing. The coffee cup shook and then steadied.

"Tampa?" he asked in a strained voice.

"No. The other."

"Don't do that to me again, you son of a bitch. I know damn well it's likely I'd be mentioned on that other deal. Let me see it."

He read both articles, tossed the paper aside. "We look better and better, lieutenant."

"That's something I want to talk about. I woke up thinking about it. You thought you recognized one of those two sharpies."

"I'm not at all sure."

"But he could have recognized you. Maybe that's why they pulled the damn fool stunt of moving in on Zaragosa in such a public place. Maybe they were going to follow him and take the money away in a more sensible place, but they recognized you with Zaragosa and knew they had to move in fast."

"So?"

"Vince, is there any remote chance they could know where you are now?"

He pinched the bridge of his nose. "Not a chance in the world. Feel better?"

"A lot better. Now the next point. Until we can split up, Vince, until you're well enough to take off, we're stuck with this situation. But when we split up, it doesn't end."

"What do you mean?"

"You're smarter than that, Vince. Suppose I goof badly and I get hauled in and asked to explain where I got a million bucks in cash. Do you think they're going to let me say I found it under a lettuce leaf? That I won it on the horses? Or I've been saving it up for a long time? They'll want to know where I went when I went away. Why I brought you back. Where you went from here, how much you had, where we got it and how. So they keep after me until I drag you into the whole thing. That means that you have a real interest in making sure I stay smart. And it works both ways. I want to be certain you're going to be smart."

He looked amused. "Jerry, I know just how I'm going to leave the country. I know where I'm going. I've got a complete new identity I'm going to step into. All I care is that you keep out of trouble for eight days after I've left here. After then, boy, you can get a sound truck and go up and down the streets telling the whole story. I won't give a damn."

"How do you expect to get the money out of the country?"

"I've got a foolproof way. That's all you have to know."

"Hell, suppose I want to get mine out too!"

He frowned. "Let me see. You don't fly a plane. So I'll give you a variation. Go to the San Diego area or the Brownsville area where we've got a contiguous water frontage setup with Mexico. Rent yourself a boat for fishing. Go down the Mexican coast, go ashore in a deserted place, stash your money where you can find it, go back and turn in your boat. Cross the border legally, go get your money and be on your way. Or, if you want a nice sensible way, go to New York. Buy bank acceptances for cash, fifteen and twenty thousand at a chunk. Hit all the banks you can manage, and then go to Boston and do the same, and Philadelphia and do the same. Sixty or seventy banks. Sixty or seventy pieces of paper. Fly to Switzerland. Customs won't give you trouble over those. Say you're on a buying trip. Open a number account in a Swiss bank. Make an investment agreement with them. When you get established some place, write them how much you want a month. Live like a king forever. Or, let me see, smuggle the cash over, if you like a gambling chance. You're a handy type. Buy a big fat American car and hide the cash in it. There are plenty of good places. Ship the car to Europe on your ticket. Or, if you want a real snap, buy diamonds. You'll take a big loss when you unload them abroad because all the smuggling traffic is the other way and nobody will be looking for them. Let me keep thinking, and I'll come up with some more. You could—"

"Okay, Vince. Okay. That's enough."

"Yesterday while I was in my most weakened condition, Jerry, your wife was trying to pump me about your plans. What you're going to do. She thought I might have talked to you. She's pretty upset, you know."

"I haven't any special plans."

"What do you want to do?'

"After you take off, I'm going to meet her terms for a divorce. I'll wait until it's final and then leave the country."

"I don't care what you do after I leave, boy, but I'm not going to want to travel for at least a week, maybe more. And I don't want her wondering why you think you don't have to work. So why don't you go back with her old man? You can quit again. But it will calm her down."

Though the idea was amazingly distasteful, I knew at once that he was right. Get back into the old pattern. Then you don't attract attention. Then people don't start wondering about you. It probably wouldn't be so bad, because I would know it was only a temporary thing.

"I'll . . . start Monday," I said.

"Good boy."

I could hear the roar of Lorraine's shower and realized I had been hearing it for some time. I talked with Vince for a little while and then went back to our bedroom. Lorraine, in orange blouse and black slacks, was leaning toward her dressing-table mirror, painting a mouth on.

"Good morning," I said.

"Hi. How's the patient?"

"I got him some coffee, but he could use some food."

"Food coming up. Scrambled eggs do you think, Jerry?"

"Should do him. And me too, if there's enough eggs. Have fun last night?"

She shrugged. "The usual crowd."

"Lorraine, honey, I've been thinking things over and I've decided to go get back in the same tired old harness tomorrow."

"Back with Daddy?" she cried with great pleasure. I nodded. "I think you're being very intelligent, Jerry. Honestly, you've had me so worried. I have to know how things stand. You know that. I just hate insecurity."

She got up and I thought she wanted to be kissed, but she evaded me, held her cheek against mine and said, "Don't muss my mouth."

I'd given in to her and so she was willing to be friendly. An uneasy truce but it was the best we could ever achieve. In all the past quarrels we had gone too far, said all the things that shouldn't have been said, tried in desperation to inflict the mortal hurt. And so made an end to our ability to hurt deeply. Now the quarrels were an empty routine, a simulated passion. It was as though we played small parts in a hit play that had gone on for years. All the cues had become automatic. We felt an almost total indifference toward each other, but we had to keep up the pretense of concern, of involvement. I remembered what Liz had said about marrying a man, and I wished that I had married a woman. But I was married to a naughty and untidy and somewhat vicious child. Mommy and Daddy were close at hand, and there was Irene for the drudgery, and the club for a playpen and the Porsche for a toy, and she could drift through all her glazed little days with glass in hand.

"Jerry, why don't you just walk down the street and tell Daddy. He's really been very upset. And you were very rude to him."

"After all he's done for me?"

She looked at me oddly. "Yes, of course."

"I was on a street corner rattling a tin cup when the Maltons came along and—"

"Leave us please not start that again. It won't hurt you to go down and tell him. They're back from church by now. And when you get back, I'll have breakfast ready."

So I walked from 118 Tyler Drive to 112 Tyler Drive and thumbed the button that started a veritable concerto of chimes. Before the last notes had died away Edith Malton came looming up out of the dimness of the hall, smelling of lavender and looking somewhat like an apprehensive and edible sea creature which swims toward the entrance of its cranny in the coral hoping to outbluff something which anticipates eating it.

She wound up her electrical whinny and told me that her Edward was in the kitchen having more coffee.

E. J. sat in his shirt sleeves, small and neat and pink and white, looking as if an indulgent mother had bathed him and combed him and knotted his tie half a dozen times until it was exactly right.

"Well, good morning, good morning, good morning," he said, rattling dishware. "Sit down. Have some coffee. Have some coffee. Edith, give Jerry some coffee."

I did it fast, hoping it would be less painful. It wasn't. "E. J., if you'll take me back, I can start to work again tomorrow."

They both beamed at me as if I'd remembered all my lines in the Christmas play. E. J. said there was no hard feelings. He said his way of doing things was the right way, and he knew that sooner or later I'd see that. He thought I had sense enough to see that. They were glad for Lorraine's sake. She'd been very upset about the whole thing. The poor kid was right in the middle. First duty to her husband, of course, but it was a nasty affair when there were quarrels in the family. We could forget all about this little difficulty. He'd charge it against my vacation. Ha ha ha. Now we'd work together and make Park Terrace the best development in this end of the state. Might be a good idea to sell the houses on Tyler Drive and move into new ones on Park Terrace.

I walked back. They had clung to me a long time.

Vince and Lorraine had finished breakfast. She had saved mine. As I was eating she came and sat opposite me in the breakfast booth and said, "Dave and Nancy Brownell are having one of those steak things again this afternoon. They asked us last Wednesday. I said I didn't know if you'd be back, but I said I'd come. They said if you got back in time, to come along."

The Brownells were on Van Dorn Road, the next street over, and so close that when we went there, we could go out the back of our house and walk through Carl Gowan's property. She said she could bring back a plate from the party to feed Vince.

We went over a little after two. The party was boiling along. About forty adults and seventy-five children. Washtubs of ice and beer, or ice and soft drinks. Though there were many of Lorraine's friends there, the group was reasonably conventional. I spotted George Farr and Cal Warder. I went over to where Tony from the club was tending an outdoor bar and got myself a deep-dish martini. And then I had some more. Maybe it was the release from the tension of Tampa and the trip. I had enough so I was rude to Cal Warder, who had tried honestly to help me, and slightly less rude to George Farr who had wanted to employ me. I was in jim-dandy shape. I ate one third of a big steak, and I went back to the house and watched Lorrie and her two best friends, Mandy Pierson and Tinker Velbiss, giggling and simpering while they clustered around Vince's bed and fed him chunks of steak, taking turns. His slow jaws ground the meat and he looked arrogant and lazy and content. I went back to the party and drank beer and switched back to gin, and passed out in a deck chair and woke up after dark, long after all the children had gone home. Samll groups were raising dismal voices in close harmony, and some clown had filled my pockets with potato chips.

Tinker found me in the darkness and cuddled with me on the deck chair. We had carried on a stylized flirtation for a long time. She said her Charlie had passed out and my Lorrie had gone on to the club with a group.

65

The bar was closed and we decided we needed a drink, so we walked two blocks to her house where Charlie had been stowed up in bed. She sent the sitter on home. We made some drinks. We sat in the dark living room and drank our drinks, and then, without plan or design, we were on the couch, drunk but dextrous, Jerry Jamison and the best red-headed girl friend his wife had ever had. It was turbulent, meaningless and competent. Then we shared a cigarette. And she had a fit of monstrous yawns. And we adjusted garments in the darkness. And she walked me to the door and we said good night in guilty whispers, and she stopped yawning long enough to kiss me, quite indifferently.

When I got home Vince was propped up, reading. He asked me to get him some cold beer and some crackers and cheese if we had any. I brought them and he told me to go swab off the lipstick. Tinker had plastered me liberally.

And I went blundering off to bed. As I was going to sleep I wondered what Vince would buy with his end of the money. And what I would buy. I wondered what I wanted. Not a succession of Tinkers, with their good but rather heavy legs and their automatic promiscuity.

Maybe what I wanted was what I had thought I was getting when I had married Lorrie.

But it was a little late for that.

Chapter 7

When I arrived at the office on Monday morning Liz was the only one there. She paused in the act of taking the plastic cover off her typewriter and looked at me with tense expectation.

I went over to her and nodded. She knew what I meant. Her face went marble white and then she blushed. She laughed nervously and said, "When do I pack?"

"Not yet. I'm coming back to work here. For a while. Not long. We'll talk later."

"Back here? But why?"

"It's a long story. Trust me."

She caught my hand and held it against her cheek and looked up at me. "That I will, Buster. This is the game that goes with the name."

E. J. came bustling in. "Good morning, good morning, good morning. A lovely day. A perfect morning in May. Come on right in, Jerry, and let's get organized."

I got out to Park Terrace by ten-thirty. It took two hours to repair some of the damage Junior had done. At twelve-thirty I sat on a pile of lumber and talked to Red Olin. Red had finished his lunch and was working on one of his big black cigars.

"I sort of had hopes you'd give me a call, Jerry. Like you said."

"I couldn't get the backing, Red. Couldn't swing it."

"I made a little list of guys to bring along. Four good boys. By Jesus, I'd like to get off this job. A man likes to keep a little self-respect. I'll be damned if I get any kind of charge building an ugly house."

I thought of the cash. "Under your hat, Red, this is just temporary, my coming back. I might still be able to work it."

"I sure hope you can."

And right then it did seem feasible. Borrow as much as I could. Feed in some of the cash very very carefully. The books would have to look right at all times. But, hell, I would be doing what I liked to do, and it was unlikely that I would go broke.

As I was trying to make myself believe that it could happen, we saw Junior drive up in his lust-red T-bird and get out, looking important. From a distance of about sixty feet, in full earshot of all the men about to get back on the job, he yelled, "Jamison, come here!"

Red grunted. I stared at the kid. He came twenty feet closer and yelled, "Come here a minute, Jerry!"

I took out a cigarette and lit it, snapped the lid on the

lighter. I said to Red, "If you can get the next five roofed, then rain won't be any problem."

"The roofers have been slow, Jerry."

Junior came marching up, his weak face working in anger, his voice thin with outrage. "What the hell's the matter with you? You heard me!"

I looked at him with mild surprise. "Why, hello, Eddie."

"When I call you, I expect you to—" but that was as far as he got. He'd come too close to me. I swung my right foot up against his chest and straightened my leg. He clutched at my foot but his fingers slipped off as he went backward, running hard. He ran into a low sand pile and went down hard and rolled all the way over it, ending up on his hands and knees on the far side, facing me. He scrambled up with a white and terrible look on his face and went stalking to his little T-bird. It rumbled flatulently and took off with him.

Red tapped the ash off his cigar and said, "Don't know how smart that was."

"Neither do I. But it was fun."

"Kind of nice to watch. He's been about to drive us nuts out here, marching around, giving orders in that squeaky voice."

"To the men?" He nodded. "You're in charge here, Red. Any orders go through you."

After I grabbed a quick lunch I went back to the office. Liz gave me a glance of warning and amusement. E. J. was so angry he no longer sounded like a French horn. He sounded like a tailgate tram.

"I understand you assaulted my son, Jamison! Explain yourself."

"Will you listen to what I say, or will you stand there and listen to what you're going to say next?"

"I am listening."

"I've been off the job a very short time, E. J. But in that time your Eddie has been very busy goofing up the operation. He's meddled with delivery schedules and quantities, tried to make dangerous structural changes in the working drawings, given conflicting orders to the men on the job. The work crews were thoroughly demoralized.

A couple of good men have quit. It will take all this week to get the job straightened out. Maybe the kid means well, but he's arrogant, inexperienced and startlingly stupid, E. J. Give him something to do that will keep him out of my hair. Today he came out and started squealing at me from a hundred feet away to come running and saluting and saying yessir, yessir. So I bounced his outraged little hind end into a sand pile and he went off in a huff. The men on the job were very pleased with the whole thing. So suppose you tell Eddie that if he comes out and tries that bigshot act again, I'll pack his mouth with wet cement."

"Who do you think you are?" E. J. brayed.

"Your general manager. You've got a sour operation going in this Park Terrace thing. You're going to lose your shirt on it, but maybe if it is run right, you can save your underwear. If Junior runs it, there are going to be little pieces of your tail scattered all over town."

"He . . . Eddie . . . is a good boy."

"Then, for God's sake, let's give him a chance to prove it. Get him a set of tools and some bib overalls and we'll fix it with the union to start him as an apprentice carpenter."

E. J. bit his lip and said, "His mother would never . . ." He caught himself, but it was too late. Those four words gave me the whole score. Too late for E. J. and much too late for Junior. I felt a sudden pity for the little man whose luck had run good for so long and was now turning thoroughly bad. As long as I had decided to work, it was easier to work hard than make a pretense of it. And I didn't have to do so much thinking about other things.

It was on Wednesday, the fourteenth of May, that I didn't get a chance to grab anything to eat until nearly three in the afternoon. I parked by a small drive-in and checked the rack outside. The morning papers were still in the rack. I hadn't finished mine at breakfast, so I took one back to a small booth. The *Vernon Examiner*. I could find no mention of the Tampa deal and only slight mention of the crushing of Melendez.

But, as I scanned an inside page, my own name

jumped out at me. It was in a local column I never read. Social gossip stuff. It was called "All Over Town" and written by a withered little ferret of a woman named Conchita Riley with dyed black hair and a collection of barbaric earrings. One of those columns where every proper name is written in upper case. I remembered that she had been at the Brownells' cook-out.

"We hear that an old war buddy of JERRY JAMISON'S is recuperating at JERRY and LORRAINE JAMISON'S charming Tyler Drive home. Your reporter didn't have a chance to meet the mysterious VINCE BISKAY, but the young marrieds who did some impromptu nurse duty last Sunday during the lawn party given by DAVE and NANCY BROWNELL report that he is a dreamboat. JERRY and VINCE were in World War II together and operated BEHIND JAPANESE LINES."

I had been eating hungrily, but it took an acute effort to swallow the last bite of hamburger. It seemed to congeal into glue in my mouth. I wondered if Lorraine had seen the column and called it to Vince's attention. He was mending rapidly but it would mean only one thing to him. No matter what shape he was in, it was time to take off. I cursed the ubiquitous Conchita Riley. Though she was a triumph of journalistic inaccuracy, this time she had managed to get the name spelled correctly. It was too much to hope that it would pass unnoticed by everybody who had read the detailed account of the Peral-Melendez thing.

I paid the check, jumped in the wagon and headed home. If Vince hadn't seen it yet, it was damn well time he did. Over a block from the entrance to Tyler Drive the wagon sputtered and died, caught again, wheezed and died with finality. The gas gauge registered less than empty. I pulled it over to the curb on its final momentum. I had meant to get gas that morning, but had forgotten.

It was about a four-minute walk to my house. The front door was open. The screen made a muted pneumatic hiss behind me. I went up the carpeted stairway and turned toward Vince's room. The door was open. But I stopped short of the door. I was halted in my tracks by an unmistakable sound. I stood there and leaned my right shoulder against the wall. I shut my jaw so tightly my teeth and muscles ached. It was a warm afternoon on Tyler Drive. A delivery truck stopped near by. A distant phone was ringing. But near at hand, not fifteen feet away, I heard a sound that was familiar, though I had never paid such specific attention to it before. Not the rhythmic surging twang of cheap springs, nor the measured squeak and creak of a cheap bed frame. This was the soft and expensive billowing pulsation of discreet and expensive bedroom hardware—a sound like a rapid sighing. I felt sweat on my body. The sounds were approaching crescendo. I made crazy word games out of it. I was not precisely a voyeur. Just listening. Oyeur, Audio infidelity. Low fidelity. When the amplifier and the speaker were perfectly matched, you had presence.

"Aaah!" she cried. "God!" she cried. "Aah!" she cried.

And soon the sound was ended. I do not know how long I stood there, chin on my chest, eyes squeezed shut. I heard her speaking to him, and I could not hear her words, but the tone was clear. Little chortling tones, smug and sated, little wheedling tones, wanting to be told how fine it all was. And a rumble of his voice. I pushed myself away from the wall and my legs felt wavery. But they held me up while I walked into the room.

He was taking a drag on a cigarette, his lazy eyes half shut. She was reaching out, trying to reach her glass on the night table without moving out of the half circle of his brown arm. Her bright blouse and slacks were a careless tangle on the floor beside the bed. Her blue eyes went staring wide and her hand knocked the drink to the floor.

She came out of bed in one sleek movement, snatching up her clothes, her face red and ugly. "You Goddamn sneak!" she screamed at me. "You filthy stinking sneak!"

She plunged by me and I turned and saw the final

glimpse of the white wobble of her traitorous buttocks as she fled toward our room. Vince had pulled the sheet across him. He lay back on the pillow, fingers laced at the back of his neck, cigarette in the corner of his mouth, watching me. I stepped closer to the bed. I stepped on a piece of ice from the melted drink and it squirted under the bed, rattled against the wall.

"You perfect bastard," I said. My voice was dry dead things rubbing together.

"How do you figure? You don't want her, Jerry boy. She made her needs pretty obvious. And it was a long boring afternoon around here. Not that she improved it a hell of a lot."

"You bastard!"

"Your record is stuck, lieutenant. Anyway, at the price I'm paying, I should get all the courtesies of the house."

"You won't be staying."

"I'm in no shape to travel yet. I'm staying."

I handed him the folded paper. My thumb marked the column. I saw his face tighten. He sat up. "Who did this?"

"How the hell do I know who did it? One of your public. Tinker Velbiss. Mandy Pierson. Maybe Lorraine. How the hell do I know who did it?"

"I can't stay here. Too much chance of some smart local reporter who reads his own paper and has a good memory. Anyway, it'll be picked up in Washington by tomorrow. And we are both going to be in a sling, my friend."

"So you got to get out of here."

"But I can't travel on my own. Jerry, you've got to find me a place. And when they come after me, you've got to do some very plausible lying. Three more days and I can take off. But right now I can just about walk. I'd attract too damn much attention."

I walked to the window and looked down on the quiet of the side yard. "I know a place. It's forty miles from here. Morning Lake. Her people have a summer camp there. In the hills. They won't go up there yet because the black flies are bad in May and June. I know where the key is. I could take you up there and lay in a stock of food. If you can do what you've just been doing, Vince, you're well enough to cook."

"I'm well enough to cook."

I turned and looked at him. He was propped up on his good elbow. "So we can knock it all off this evening. We'll split the money. I'll get you settled. You move on when you're well enough, and leave the place just as you found it. And I hope to God I never have to look at you again."

"How do I get out of there when I'm well enough to travel?"

"The camp is two miles from the village. We go through the village to get there. You can get a bus there."

"It sounds all right to me."

I looked at him steadily. "But this is extra service, Vince."

It took him but a moment to catch on. "I'll return your compliment. You bastard. How much?"

"One more brick of hundreds for the extra service."

"Your help comes damn high."

"And one more brick in payment for services rendered . . . by my wife."

"What does that make you, Jerry boy?"

"The most successful pimp in the county."

"You're harder than I thought you were. It makes it one of the most expensive little romps in the hay in history."

"You can get along on what you'll have left. If you try hard."

"What if I say no?"

"Then maybe I take off and you can stay right here. Maybe when I take off I won't count so good. I might make a bad mistake."

He lounged back, rolling off his elbow and his hand went under the pillow and came out with a dwarf automatic. It had a foreign look to it. It was utterly steady, and aimed at my belt buckle. "You could make a hell of a bad mistake."

73

I grinned at him. "Where was that when you needed it?"

"In my hip pocket, but I needed two hands to hold up Zaragosa and I never got a chance to go for it. And when I was in the back of your wagon I had it in my hand until I was damn sure you weren't going to get cute. Then I put it in my suitcase."

"Trusting old Vince."

"It's Jap. Recent. They're making some nice ones now."

"How stupid do you think I am, Vince? How easy do you think I scare? Fire the silly damn thing and then figure out what you do next."

"You get more professional every day," he said. He put it away. "Okay. You and sweet Lorraine earn a hundred thousand more. I better get out of here while I still own the suitcase."

"Get yourself dressed and packed up. We'll take off as soon as we can make it."

I went down the hall. Our bedroom door was locked. I knocked and called to her but she didn't answer. In the garage I found a can of gas for the power mower, gas that hadn't yet had the oil mixed into it. As I started down the street with the can, I met Irene walking from the bus.

I said, "Irene, Mrs. Jamison isn't feeling well. She won't want anything to eat, and I'll eat out."

"Well, there was some ironing . . ."

"Can it wait until tomorrow?"

"I guess so."

"Come on along. I'll drive you back to where you can get a bus quicker."

"Ran out of gas, huh? Thought I recognized the station wagon back there."

I dumped the gas in the tank. After I turned it over a dozen times with the starter, it caught. I drove Irene to her bus stop, told her we would expect her in the morning. She got out and looked at me with a curious intensity and said, "Mr. Jamison, you take it to the Lord in prayer."

"I'll do that, Irene."

74

"There's nothing can't be eased by prayer. You get down on your knees and pray to Him."

"Thanks, Irene." She turned toward the bus stop. I circled back to the gas station, thinking about her. I wondered how much she saw, how much she knew, and how much she was able to guess.

When the tank was filled I signed the slip and went back to the house and parked in the drive. For once Lorraine had put the Porsche in its stall. I went up and tried the bedroom door again. Still locked. Vince sat on the bed fully dressed, his right arm in the sling inside his coat, loose sleeve tucked neatly in the side pocket, straw hat at a rakish angle. I carried his suitcase. He managed to get down the stairs by himself, backing down so he could hold the railing with his good hand, and taking one stair at a time on his stiff left leg. It made him look white around the mouth, but he made it. I hoped it hurt as badly as it seemed to.

He sat in the kitchen while I went down to the coal bin. This time I used work gloves to unstack the wood. When the suitcase was cleared I opened it and took out twenty-nine bundles of hundreds and tucked them neatly into the place where the suitcase had been. I restacked the wood and threw the work gloves aside and carried the suitcase back up to the kitchen. It was considerably lighter and easier to manage.

"I suppose you want to check."

"If it isn't too much trouble."

"Suppose she comes down?"

"I don't think she will, and neither do you."

I opened it. He counted it carefully. "Okay."

He put his dark glasses on and we went to the car. He got in awkwardly. I put the two bags in the back. I could have driven through town, but I took the long way around. It was just six o'clock when I turned off the narrow county road into the driveway that dropped steeply down to the lakeshore camp. I knew the camp well. E. J. had built it right after he and Edith were married. And he had done a damn good job. He had built it to last. In the first couple of summers of our marriage

Lorraine and I had gone up there whenever we could. I remembered one hot August night when we were alone in the camp. We had been to a barn dance in the village. At about three in the morning, under a full moon, we'd gone skinny-dipping in the black water of the lake. I remembered how whitely she had gleamed in the water, remembered carrying her up to the camp, to the big old double bed, dripping wet and shivering deliciously in my arms.

I wondered where and why it had all gone so wrong.

"A revolting name," Vince said.

E. J. had named it Sootsus. I had become so accustomed to the name that I had forgotten how sickening it was.

I parked in the turnaround behind the camp. I carried the two bags to the shallow porch, put them down and went over and got the key from its usual place tucked behind an edge of the windowframe.

"When you leave, put the key back there."

"Righto."

I brought in the cardboard carton of groceries I had bought on the way up. I found the fuse box and closed the two knife switches and said, "Yank the power off when you leave."

"Check."

"Try to stay out of sight. It's pretty secluded, but some of the neighbors might be in early. Don't light it up like a church at night."

"Okay."

I couldn't think of anything else. I turned to say good-by. He was leaning heavily against the kitchen table, the little Jap automatic pointed at my chest.

"What the hell?"

"Good-by and all that," he said. "I just don't want you any closer than you are right now. You are getting too cute and too hungry too fast, Jerry. And there's a hell of a lot of money in the next room, and that is a deep lake. So we carried it off, and this is the end of it. For some funny reason I don't trust you any more. I don't trust you at all. So don't get some cute ideas and try to come back here, Jerry."

"It never entered my head."

"But it might. Don't be tempted. *Adiós, amigito.*"

"And good-by and bad luck to you, bastard."

And I marched out and drove off, gunning the wagon up the steep drive, feeling it weave as the rear wheels slipped. I was back home a little before seven. Dusk was on its way. The heat bugs sang in the elms and fancy plantings of Tyler Drive.

A half tray of ice cubes were melting in the kitchen. Smoke wreathed upward from a smoldering lipsticked butt. I listened in the upstairs hall. The bedroom radio was on. The door was locked. I went down and used the melting ice with enough bourbon to fill a tall glass. I wandered upstairs with the tall glass. I went into the guest room. I looked at the rumpled bed. I picked up the glass she had knocked over. A piece as big as half a silver dollar had been knocked out of the rim. There was a damp stain on the dark blue rug.

You can be reasonably certain of something, and yet have the ability to force it out of your mind, to tell yourself it never really happened, it was just your imagination and jealousy.

But not this time.

Not this unmistakable time.

And I didn't know why it should hurt so badly. I had thought I was out of love with her, completely. It shouldn't hurt this way. Not this sick shame and pain that makes you want to drive your fist into the wall.

Anyway, what did I have to kick about? Wasn't this just another Tyler Drive pastime? Did I think the quickie with Tinker was epochal or something? The saucy goose deserves a propaganda. So Vince rolled in the hay with a bored, petulant, spoiled housewife who was making the most of her looks before alcohol took the last of her freshness and prettiness. It shouldn't mean any more to me than it did to Vince. Or to her.

I finished the bourbon. It was getting to me. I made another one. I went and knocked on the bedroom door.

I knocked and knocked. She opened it. She stood swaying in a flowered robe, and looked at me with blurred face, sneering expression and said, "So come in, if you're so damn anxious."

And I went in.

Chapter 8

I walked directly across the bedroom and sat down on her dressing table bench heavily, so heavily some of the bourbon slopped out onto the back of my hand and wrist.

"Lover boy is gone," I said.

She peered at me. "What do you mean, gone?"

"Did you expect him to stay?"

"He's too sick to go. Where'd he go? Wha'd you do with Vince?"

"Took him to the airport."

"Where is he going?"

"I didn't ask. You want to follow him?"

"I might just as well follow him as stay here. With a damn sneaky sneak."

"I tell you I did not sneak."

She sat on the foot of her bed, facing me. "You did so sneak. I would have heard the car. I was listening."

"I ran out of gas about two blocks away."

"A likely story. A *very* likely story!"

"You can ask Irene. I met her while I was carrying gas back to the car. I drove her back to the main bus stop."

She squinted her eyes at me. "You really ran outa gas?"

"Yes."

"Then it was just bad luck. Just stinking bad luck, thass all."

She looked like a guilty and rebellious child. "Lorraine."

"Yeah?"

"Lorraine, honey, why do you make such a mess of everything? Why do you drink yourself stupid? Why did you do that today with Vince?"

She made a helpless gesture with her free hand. "Why do people do anything? It wouldn't hurt anything, would it? He wouldn't say anything. I wouldn't say anything. So what's the harm in a little fun?"

The bourbon had made me feel very solemn, quite pontifical.

"That is an immoral attitude," I said.

"You're a stuffy bassar, aren't you?"

"Why do you drink so much?"

"Because I like to drink so much. That's why I drink so much. And what'd you send Irene home for? I'm hungry."

"Lorraine, honey, we ought to try to understand each other better."

"Go ahead. Understand me. Tell me what I'm like. You caught me, didn't you. Gives you a big free ticket to give me a big free lecture. Go ahead. You caught me. It makes me feel kind of ashamed you caught me, but you ought to feel good. Forgive the poor sinner. Say prayers maybe. Like Irene."

"Don't be so defensive. I'm trying to talk calmly."

"Be calm and superior."

"That's the point. I'm not superior. I . . . I haven't been faithful either."

"Now you admit it! That washed-out Liz Addams. I knew it all the time, but you kept denying—"

"Not Liz Addams, Lorraine. Your friend Tinker."

"Tinker!" she gasped. "Where? When?"

"Last Sunday. After dark. In her house."

She looked at me with complete shock and consternation. I expected her to break into tears. And she broke into an uncontrollable fit of giggling.

"Oh my God. Tinker! Oh, brother. Oh, the fun I'm going to have with her."

"Shut up!" I yelled at her. "You're not even human!"

She stood up, wavering and snickering, and headed for the bathroom. I ran after her and caught her by the arm at the doorway. "What's wrong with you?" I yelled into her face. "You ought to see a psychiatrist. You've got some kind of a disease. You act as if . . . adultery was some kind of a game."

She wrenched her arm free and looked up at me. "Well, of *course*," she cooed. "Of *course*, darling. It is a game. A wonnerful, wonnerful game." She unbelted her robe so that it hung apart, did an ugly parody of a bump and grind and said, "Soon's I see a dog about a girl, we'll make ourselves comfy and exchange names. I bet I win. I got a hell of a long list. Ooooh, brother, have I ever got a long list."

I looked down into the filth of her face and the filth of her smile and the filth of her eyes. And called her the foulest name that came to mind. She raked my face with her nails. I put my right hand on the side of her face and thrust her into the bathroom with all my strength.

It was a floor-length robe when it was belted. It hung longer at the sides when unbelted. I believe that the first involuntary step she took, the first sideways step was onto the hem of the robe. It tripped her perfectly so that she left her feet completely, turning in the air slightly toward her own left so that she had no chance of getting her hands in front of her. The tub is in direct line with the doorway. Her head struck the tub with such a terrible force that it rang like a great muffled gong. She lay on her back with her head turned too far to the side, at a sickening and impossible angle. Her nails scrabbled listlessly at the tiled floor. Her body tensed in a great rippling shudder, then collapsed into a stillness and smallness. Her eyes were half open. She looked small as a child. And with a dreadful stillness. The bright fluorescence of the bathroom lights made it all a special horror. My only instinct was to turn the light out. The last gray of the day was at the window.

I went back into the bedroom. I sat at her dressing table and looked in the mirror. I was breathing with great shuddering breaths and suddenly I could hear in the room the rasping noise of my own breath. I saw the three scratches on my cheek. The middle one was longest and deepest. A single drop of blood ran from the middle gouge down to the angle of my jaw. It clung there, drying. In the mirror I saw the drink in my hand. I set it aside.

Then I knew that of course I had been wrong. Knocked her out. That's all. In a little while she'd come wobbling out, cursing me.

So I went into the bathroom and knelt carefully on the tile and laid my ear on her chest, knowing I would hear the slow thump of her heart. And heard a monstrous silence.

I went back into the bedroom and snatched up my drink, then put it down again. I crossed to the bedroom phone on her night stand and sat on her bed and picked up the phone. I heard the dial sound. I listened to it for several seconds. You dialed zero. Then you asked for the police. Then you said, I just sort of pushed her a little.

I hung up the phone and dried the palms of my hands on her bedspread.

Think, damn it! Pull yourself up out of the liquor stupor and the shock and start thinking. She is dead. Gone. Finished. *Muerto*. A stiff, a cadaver—something for the meat wagon, the embalming fluid and some organ music.

Take your choice, Jamison. Phone the cops right now and take a chance on some justice and mercy and maybe a minimum of three years for manslaughter. Or bitch up the evidence and take a chance on getting out whole.

And how about the money under the wood pile?

And what about the questions that are going to be asked about Vincente Biskay?

Get cold, Jamison. Get cold and logical and objective. And think. Think of all the angles.

Bar of soap on the floor. Rub some on the bottom of her foot. Press it against the tile and make a long smear of soap. Leave water running in the sink. Get the hell out. Establish an alibi. Come back and find her.

But they'd have some cute ideas about the angle of the fall, the force, the way the soap should have skidded. Might be worth a try if she hadn't gouged you. They'll clean under her fingernails, dig out the little flecks of tissue she tore out of your cheek, and find enough blood to type.

Start the big run tonight. Take the cash and start moving fast.

And then they'll really be after you. No, you have to leave clean. Be trouble enough without that kind of pressure.

Be so much better if she could leave.

And that idea had a curious flavor of plausibility about it. I turned it around and around to see where and how it would fit.

And made it fit.

A big affair with Vince. A quarrel. (That was when she gouged me.) And then the two of them ran away together.

It would fit Vince's history. And her reputation.

But I couldn't go off half cocked. I had to sit and go over every aspect, and build a plan, and check the plan from every direction, from every angle.

And as I was beginning to sell myself on it, I happened to remember something that would make it perfect. Might make it perfect. If I could find it. If the wording was right. If it was the way I remembered it.

Way back in the marriage when the quarrels had been violent, when it had hurt when she had savaged me, before our scenes had become routine, there had been one particularly unpleasant quarrel. I could not even remember what it was about but she had left me forever. When I came home from work I had found her note. She had scrawled it on the flyleaf of a book I had been reading, had left the book propped open in the middle of the living room rug for me to find.

I went downstairs. It took a few minutes to find the book. I remembered that after we had made our fragile peace, she had wanted to cut the flyleaf out, but I had decided to keep it. I remembered having the vague idea that it might become useful ammunition in the event of another quarrel.

I took the book over to the lamp and read in her slanty green-ink scrawl, the i's dotted with little circles:

"Jerry—This is no damn good for either of us. I'm leaving for good this time. Don't try to find me. I won't be back." It was signed with one initial, a sprawling L.

I could not remember that anyone else knew of the note. I remembered that I had read of scientific methods which could determine the age of ink. This had been written over six years ago. But it looked crisp and fresh.

I heard footsteps on the front porch and slapped the book shut, slid it into its space on the shelf. My heart was beating heavily.

I went to the door. I did not turn the porch light or hall light on. I was relieved to see that it was a woman silhouetted against the street light.

"Jerry?"

"Hi, Mandy."

"Lorraine around?"

"No, she isn't."

"Our damn phone is out of order again. That's the third time this month. Know where I can find her?"

"She didn't say where she was going. She didn't take her car, so she's probably somewhere in the neighborhood."

"Well, I don't feel like tramping all over looking for her. If she gets back before ten have her try to call me and if it's still out of order maybe she could drive over for a couple of minutes."

"I'll tell her."

"Thanks, Jerry."

I watched her go down the steps. I went back and got the book and took it upstairs and got a razor blade and cut the flyleaf out neatly. I took the book back down and replaced it. Back in the bedroom I propped the note up against her dressing table mirror. It looked plausible, and it was entirely accurate. She wouldn't be back.

I went down to the storeroom in the cellar. The lawn chairs were stacked there. They hadn't been put out yet. They were covered by a tarp. I pulled it off and held it up. It was big enough, a khaki tarp with a few tears and grease stains.

I took the tarp and some heavy twine up to the bathroom. I turned on the light. I had expected her to look different somehow, but she looked the same. I spread the tarp out on the tile floor beside her. I sat on my heels and wiped my palms on the thighs of my slacks. It was several moments before I could make up my mind to touch her. Then I reached over and grasped her by the left shoulder and the hip and rolled her onto the tarp. Her body had changed. She was not cold, but neither did she have the warmth of life. It was a middle temperature, queasy and unlikely. I rolled her over one more half turn so that she was once again on her back. I put her arms at her sides and her ankles together. I folded the tarp up over her legs and down over her face. Then I tucked the tarp around her. I passed the twine under her and tied the bundle firmly at ankles, knees, thighs, waist, bust and throat. When I stood up my knees were trembling. Only then did I realize that I had somehow managed it all without once looking directly at her face.

I picked the long bundle up awkwardly. I had heard that the dead are unexpectedly heavy. But she was no heavier than on the many other occasions when I had had to carry her after she had passed out. I half stood her against the wall as I had done so many times before, then bent over, put my right shoulder against her belly and grasped her around the knees, straightening up as the upper part of her body fell forward against my back.

As I stood up she made a ghastly croak of complaint. I felt an instantaneous cold sweat on every part of my body. I stood with the weight of her on my shoulder and told myself that it was merely the captured air being forced out of dead lungs. I took her down the dark stairs and out to the kitchen and lowered her to the floor, easing her down gently. I locked all three outside doors and ran back upstairs. I mopped the bathroom floor, and then did all I could to make the gouges on my right cheek less conspicuous, finding and using the pancake makeup Lorraine used to cover blemishes.

Just as I had finished the phone rang. I hurried into

the bedroom, sat on the bed, let it ring twice more while I brought my breathing under control.

"Hello?"

"Jerry, Mandy again. Sorry to be a nuisance. Lorraine in yet?"

"Not yet."

"Well, tell her our phone is working again."

"I . . . I have to go out in a few minutes, Mandy. I may be late getting back. But I'll leave her a note."

"How about me coming over and staying with your sick friend if you're both out?"

"No need of that. Anyway, Vince is asleep. Thanks, Mandy."

"Is he receptive to blondes?"

"Very. And brunettes and redheads."

"You wouldn't be just a teeny weeny little bit receptive to redheads yourself, would you, Jerry dear?"

"What do you mean?"

"Well, I heard that you and . . . a mutual friend were observed having a very torrid little time in a deck chair recently. And then you both slunk off into the bulrushes."

"A case of mistaken identity."

"I'm sure it must have been. Well, you leave that note, dear."

"I will."

I hung up. I went down to the living room, sat at the small desk and wrote, "Lorrie—When you come in Mandy wants you to phone her. The patient is sound asleep. I'm going out. I don't know when I'll be back. That nasty little threat of yours has made me restless. I keep hoping you didn't mean it."

I signed it. I took it into the dark kitchen, put it on the edge of the breakfast booth table, weighted it down with a salt shaker. I looked at the shadowy bundle on the floor near the door and said, "Mandy wants you to phone, darling." And then I laughed, and stopped abruptly. It was a creaky laugh, twisted and nervous and horrible.

I went to the garage, put a shovel in the back of the wagon, backed it out, turned around, backed it into the driveway and lowered the tailgate. I waited for several moments in the darkness. The neighborhood was quiet. I looked at the luminous dial of my watch. Twenty minutes to ten. I could hear no car coming, no pedestrian sounds. I went and got her. I picked her up as before and ran heavily with her to the station wagon. I sat her on the tailgate, pushed her over backward. Her head thumped hard. I picked up her legs and slid her in beside the shovel, and covered the tell-tale shape of the twine-wrapped bundle with the old army blanket I keep in the back of the wagon. The shape was still too evident. I pulled the blanket off, laid the shovel across her and covered her again. It made an awkward and meaningless bundle.

I locked the house and drove carefully into the city. I parked the wagon on a quiet side street behind the Hotel Vernon and locked it. I went into the bar. It was a quiet evening. Four or five couples and three men at the bar. I sat on a stool. Timmy came to my end of the bar and said, "Good evening, Mr. Jamison."

"Is it?" I said, scowling at him and slurring my words. "Gimme a bourbon mist, Timmy." I put a five on the bar.

When he brought it I said, "Hellova world, Timmy. Can't live with 'em and can't live without 'em."

"That's the way it goes sometimes, Mr. Jamison."

Lorraine had made a spectacle of herself just often enough in the Hotel Vernon bar so that Timmy had a look of genuine compassion.

"I'll be damned if I'll go home. Maybe I'll get a room here."

"These things blow over," he said.

I drank my drink and left him a dollar tip. I wanted him to remember me. I lurched into the door frame with my shoulder as I left. I walked quickly to the car and drove to our new development, Park Terrace. And for once I had cause to be thankful for E. J.'s marble-headed stubbornness. Time after time I had pleaded with him to employ a night watchman. I had pointed out that petty pilferage off the job and malicious damage by kids was costing us more than a watchman would cost. But he would say that the men could lock up their tools in the shacks, and you couldn't keep kids from stealing scrap lumber.

I knew that on the following morning the transitmix trucks would be out to pour footings, foundation walls and the carport slabs for the next ten houses. The forms were in. I parked beside a high stack of cinderblock. I walked around until my eyes were used to the night light. I had to make certain our development hadn't been chosen on this night of a half moon by anybody with romance in mind. The nearest occupied houses were a quarter of a mile away. I watched a commercial airliner settling toward the airport, running lights blinking. Two distant cats were enchanting each other with horrid sounds.

I got the shovel and stepped over the taut string and the edge of the form for a slab and picked a place about three feet from the edge. The drain would go in the middle. I had selected a house where the slope of the lot had caused us to use fill on the carport side of the house, so the digging was relatively easy. I worked hard and fast. My wind went rapidly and my back and shoulders began to ache. Though I had intended to go deeper, when I was down about four feet, I quit.

With the lights out, I backed the wagon as close as I could. I lowered the tailgate, pulled on her ankles, then pulled her up into a sitting position and took her on my shoulders again. In the length and width the hole was a tight fit. I consciously tried to dull my awareness of what I was doing as I shoveled the dirt back in. Once the mound was high over her, I had to force myself to the point where I could endure stamping it down. I thought of her in the sun by a poolside, thought of her in a formal dress, her shoulders bare. I saw her walking and running and laughing.

There was less excess dirt than I had expected. I guess she did not displace very much. What there was I threw down the slope with wide swings of the shovel. I used the khaki blanket to brush away the evidence of my stamping.

Eleven o'clock. Time was going too fast. I drove home, put the shovel away, went to the big hall closet upstairs and got out her two large suitcases. I packed her things. I tried to select what she would select. The best. The newest. Suits, skirts, blouses, shoes, underwear, jewelry, perfume, cosmetics. And I did it in a hasty sloppy way as she might have done it, leaving drawers open and clothing on her closet floor.

When I was nearly finished the phone rang. I let it ring. It rang eleven times before the caller gave up. I took the suitcases down and put them in the luggage space behind the bucket seats of the little copper-colored Porsche. I wedged her mink cape in between the suitcases. I put the convertible top up on the little car. As usual, she had left the key in the ignition. I went back into the house. When I came out again, I had changed to old hunting pants, tennis shoes and a dark wool shirt. I carried her purse, and I carried the .22 calibre target pistol I had not touched in at least three years. The nine-shot clip was fully loaded.

As with Vince, I circled the city until I could strike the Morning Lake road, Route 167, and turn north. The little car, the unfortunately conspicuous little car, droned north up into the hills. It clung beautifully on the corners. I was worried about being spotted when I went through the village of Brindell, two miles from Morning Lake. I need not have worried. A dozen dim street lights, a few dark stores, a cluster of dark houses. In the middle of the village I turned off Route 167 on the unnumbered county road. The night was so still I thought Vince might be alerted if I tried to stop too close to the driveway, so I turned the key off a quarter of a mile or more away and let it drift as far as it would before turning it off onto the steep grassy shoulder under the tree shadows.

It did not seem possible that I had been at the camp just that afternoon. I could more easily believe that I had driven Vince up days ago. I worked the slide on the automatic, jacking a bullet into the chamber. I left it on full cock, but kept my forefinger in front of the trigger guard in case I should slip on a loose stone in the driveway.

Where the moon came down between the trees to shine on the drive I could walk confidently, avoiding twigs and loose stones. Where the leaves were thick overhead I had to take shorter steps, testing each step carefully before bringing my full weight onto it. Once a loose stone rattled against another. I stood and held my breath and listened. I was being consumed by black flies. I could hear the lap of the lake against the rocks along the shore and against the piling of the dock. A dog barked, far far away. And somewhere behind me an owl asked who.

This was work I had done long ago, work I had learned to do quietly, efficiently and well. When at last I came to the end of the drive I went down on one knee and studied the black bulk of the camp against the moon silver of the lake and an angle of starry sky. I went over the floor plan in my memory, and guessed that he would select the bedroom in the southeast corner of the building. It was the handiest, and held a large double bed. I picked up half a dozen walnut-sized stones in my left hand. I could smell the sharp-sweet odor of gun lubricant.

I crossed the open moonlit space of the turnaround quickly and silently and flattened myself against the rough siding of the building. The expectation of being stopped by a bullet as I crossed that space had taken my breath away. After several moments I moved again, moved along the side of the building until I stood close beside the window of the southeast bedroom. And I could hear his breath, slow and heavy in sleep. I stepped a little away from the building and threw one of the stones off into the woods. It pattered through the leaves and struck a branch with a sharp sound and fell to the ground. After the second stone I listened and could no longer hear the breathing. I threw a third and then waited. I heard a soft creak of the bed. I heard a squeak of a floorboard under his weight. I put my finger lightly on the trigger.

When I judged that he had time to reach the window

I stepped out in front of it, raising the pistol as I did so. His face was a paleness against the blackness of the room, and about three feet above me.

I fired three shots into the center of that pale oval blur, then fell flat and rolled tightly against the side of the building. And I heard him come down onto the wooden floor, heard the long rumbling fall, thuds of bone on wood, and a sharper sound of metal on wood, and a heavy grunt, and a dwindling sigh. I waited ten minutes by my watch. I used the pistol barrel to poke a hole in the copper screen in the middle near the bottom member of the frame. I put my finger through, pushed the hook out of the eye, pried the frame outward and lifted it off the top hooks, set it against the side of the house, without once getting my head in front of the screen. I reached gun and lighter into the room and snapped the lighter on. I looked at him quickly. I put the lighter back in my pocket, pulled myself up and climbed into the room. I pulled the shades and turned on the light. He was in his underwear. He lay half on his side with his face against the floor, one leg doubled under him. I put my heel against his shoulder and rolled him over. He rolled loosely. He had taken one in the upper lip, one close beside his nose on the left side, and one in the corner of his eye. The hydraulic action of hollowpoints on brain fluid had grotesquely altered the shape of his head, bulging it badly at the temples. He had bled very little. Had I been using long rifle shells it would have blown his head apart.

I left the light on, let myself out through the locked door. I collected his belongings, packed them in his bag—after taking out the fat stack of hundreds and stuffing them in my pockets—and wedged the bag in with Lorraine's things. There seemed no point in trying to dress him. It would be a waste of the time that was growing dangerously short. I took his wrists and dragged him to the door and out across the shallow porch, then got him into the passenger seat in the car. It was an infuriating struggle. I went in and checked to see if I had forgotten anything of his. I found his razor on the shelf in the crude bathroom. I took it out and hurled it far out into the lake. The black metal suitcase was under the bed. I looked inside. The money was there. I took my pistol and the Jap automatic down onto the dock and threw them out into the lake and listened to the noise they made. Like stones. Thirty feet from the end of the short dock, the lake floor shelves off steeply.

I got into the car and pushed him over so that he slumped against the window, the closed window. I knew the precise place to go. The county road follows the lake shore. Half a mile east of the camp, it practically overhangs the lake. I knew the spot well. E. J. and I had fished for bass there, in the late summer when the water is warm and the bass are deep. You can't anchor. You tie up to one of the bushes that cling to the sheer rock wall. Cars go by fifteen feet over your head, and you fish in seventy feet of water. They say it used to be a good place for lakers before they were all fished out.

I saw but one lighted camp along the lake shore. When I came to the spot, I turned off motor and lights and got out and looked the situation over. The barrier along the edge of the drop-off was of concrete posts and heavy cable. I had forgotten how extensive the barrier was. I began to feel terribly afraid that it was going to be impossible. But when I walked to the far end I saw how it could be done. There was room to drive the little car off the road and around the end of the fence. And there was a flat space on the wrong side of the fence that gradually became narrower until it was too narrow for the car, but by then it was over the deep water. I drove the car around and as far as I dared. I put the lights off. I left the motor running, left it out of gear. I squeezed out through the small space left when I opened my door against the fence. I held on to the fence with one hand, reached back in and banged the lever up with the heel of my hand, forcing it into low. The car bucked but did not stall and began to crawl. I slammed the door on my side. It moved forward in the night. It passed me. When it was fifteen feet beyond me, the right front wheel dropped, and dirt and loose stones fell to the water below. I thought for a moment it would cling there. The motor had stalled. Then it tipped farther, quite slowly, and then suddenly it went. I leaned out. It landed upside down and sent out a sheet of spray that was white in the weak moonlight. It seemed to hesitate on the surface, and then the water closed over it. I could hear the waves it had made running along the shore line, disappearing in the distance. Bubbles broke on the surface. The roiled water gradually became still.

As I climbed over the fence I heard a car coming. I ran across the road and up the steep slope, scrabbling up on my hands and knees. I sat there. A pickup truck sped by at a dangerous speed and rattled away into the distance.

I slid back down and walked back to Camp Sootsus. I scrubbed up the few blood spots. I thumbed the copper screening back together so that the holes were small and inconspicuous. I carried the carton of groceries far into the woods and left it there, cursing myself for forgetting to put it in the car. At twenty after two I crawled under the camp, dragging the tin suitcase. I worked it around in front of me and pushed it far back, completely out of sight.

I turned out the lights after closing all the windows and making up the bed Vince had slept in. I locked the door, put the key in its proper place on the window sill, and walked up the drive.

I made the two miles back to the village as quickly as I could, trotting until my wind was gone, and then walking until I had stopped wheezing, and then trotting again. I walked through the village. Dogs barked. When I was beyond the village, I began trotting again. Each time I heard a car coming behind me, I turned and walked backward, frantically thumbing a ride. It was three-thirty when the truck stopped for me, a big green tractor trailer combo. I climbed up into the cab. There was a stunted wiry little man at the big wheel.

"Kinda late for walking, pal."

"Thanks a lot for stopping. I'm going to Vernon."

"First place we come to, pal," he said, working the

big rig up through the gears. "Like I said, it's late for walking."

"It sure is. You see, it's like this. I got to be in Vernon early in the morning. They thought they could get my old pickup truck fixed back there in the village in plenty of time, and I was helping work on it, but then the others quit and I was working on it alone and I figured I could get it going but along about an hour ago I plain give up on her and figured I'd better figure out some other way of getting down to Vernon to meet my wife coming in on the early train so she won't be worried or anything, and by then it was too late to get anybody to drive me on in and I couldn't get the lend of a car from anybody on account of I had hard luck and racked up a couple cars a while back and I couldn't get no bus connection this time of night so I figured I'd start out hitching and nobody else, going like hell, showed any sign of stopping until you come along and I sure am thankful to you and I guess now I'll be able to get a little sitting-up kind of sleep in the railroad station."

"Oh," he said.

He let me off a mile and a half from Tyler Drive at a few minutes after four. I let myself into the house at quarter after. By half past I had cleaned myself up and changed back to the same clothing I had worn when I had stopped in the bar at the Hotel Vernon. I felt stupefied by exhaustion. I mixed a monster drink of Scotch and belted it down and felt it hit bottom. I dribbled a little from the bottle on the front of my jacket.

At twenty minutes of five, with the green-ink note in my hand, I went onto E. J.'s front porch. I put my thumb on the bell and kept it there. I kicked the front door heavily and constantly. And I did a little yelling.

Chapter 9

When E. J. swung the front door open, his little blue eyes were popping sparks at me and his face was blotched with angry red. His white hair was tousled, and he wore a baggy little gray robe. My mother-in-law was halfway down the front stairs clutching a shiny purple robe around her and looking angry and alarmed.

"Stop this damn racket at once!" E. J. roared at me. "At once. You'll wake up this whole half of the city, damn it. What's wrong? You're drunk."

I rocked from side to side and leered at him. "Not so damn drunk I can't read, pops."

"Can't read! Can't read? What the hell has that got to do with anything?"

"See'f you can read, daddyo," I said and handed him Lorraine's note.

He turned it toward the light. His lips moved as he read it. He glanced sideways at his wife and said, "You better come in, Jerry." His tone was different.

Edith Malton came heavily down the rest of the stairs and said, "What is this? What is happening?" She snatched the note away from E. J. She read it at a glance. "What have you done to my little girl?" she wailed.

I wobbled into the living room and collapsed into a chair and looked at them blearily.

"Make him some strong coffee, Edie," E. J. ordered.

"I will not. Not until I find out what happened."

"It's just a little spat," E. J. said.

"Not a spat. An equation, pops. A plus B equals C, D and E."

He sat on the arm of the couch and looked at me bleakly. "See if you can pull yourself together, Jerry. It sounds as if Lorrie has left you."

"She sure has."

"Did you have a fight? What happened to your face?"

"She gouged me, E. J."

"Why?"

"Know about the house guest? Know about my old war buddy, Vince?"

"Lorraine mentioned him," Edith said very coldly.

"Came home early this afternoon. Hell, yesterday afternoon. What time is it, anyway?"

"Nearly five o'clock in the morning, son," E. J. said.

"Well, I came home about three in the afternoon. Maybe a little later. Car ran out of gas down around the corner."

"I saw you go by with a can of gas later on," Edith said. "I wondered what the trouble was. Wasn't Irene with you?"

"Yes. Stopped her from going to the house. Didn't want her there. It was a mess."

"Just what do you mean?" E. J. said.

"Hate to have to say this. But I better. Car ran out of gas. I wasn't spying on anybody. Never entered my mind. Found Lorraine in bed with Vince."

Edith gave a squeak of pure outrage and disbelief. "That is a vile lie!" she said. "Our Lorrie would never never—"

"Shut up!" E. J. brayed. "Then what?"

"There was, you might say, a fight, E. J. A big old battle. I got gouged. I wanted to kill the both of them. But I didn't. Lorraine locked herself in the bedroom. I couldn't beat up on Vince. He's still too weak from his operation. I had a couple of drinks. I didn't go back to work."

"I wondered about that," E. J. said. "You usually check in at the office before you go home."

"Didn't even think of it. Too upset. I stormed out and had a few drinks here and there and then I went back. Vince was asleep. Lorraine wasn't home. Mandy Pierson stopped by. She was trying to get in touch with her. I don't know what for. I left a note for her to call Mandy. When we fought she said she was going to leave for good. I thought it was bluff. I got restless and went out again. Vince was still sleeping. I went down to the hotel and had a drink. Then I drove around, trying to get things straightened out in my mind. You know. I got home a little while ago."

"Dead drunk," Edith said.

"Will you kindly shut up!" E. J. roared at her.

"Well, I got home and I found that note you've got, Edith. She's gone. Her car is gone. All her good clothes and jewelry are gone. And my old buddy is gone too. Bag and baggage. She took off with him. That's the equation I was telling you about. They ran off together in her car."

E. J. looked very troubled. There was silence in the room. Edith said, "Humphf! The whole thing is a tissue of lies. Our little Lorrie would never never . . ."

And I was suddenly very tired of that. I said, "Listen to me a minute. I'll tell you what your Lorrie will do and won't do. Your precious delicate little Lorrie. She's been a lush for five years and she's been getting worse. You people haven't admitted that to yourselves, but in your hearts you know it. You've seen it. She spends all day every day with a glass in her hand."

"Whose fault is that?" Edith demanded.

"Yours, maybe. I married her too damn fast. I didn't know her, and I didn't do any checking. Maybe you think that during her college days she was the campus queen. One of her college pals got stoned one night at our house and I got the word. She was the college pushover, Miss Campus Roundheels. How many times do you think I've had to go find her in parked cars at parties or at the club and yank her out, all smeared up with her lipstick, clothes all rumpled, tipsy and silly and disgusting?"

"Never!" Edith said.

E. J. looked at her. He suddenly looked a hell of a lot older. "Jerry knows what he's talking about, Edie. I've known it too."

Her long face sagged and she looked like a tired and overworked horse. "Couldn't you control your wife?" she asked.

"Couldn't you raise a daughter? Hell, this doesn't get

96

us any place. This just happens to be the first time I caught her in bed."

"Was she . . . clothed?" E. J. asked in a strained voice.

"She was naked as an egg."

"Oh."

I pushed myself to my feet. "Well, she's gone. It probably could have waited until morning. But I thought you ought to know. I'm not going to look for her. She can stay gone."

"You never loved her," Edith said.

I looked at her for a few moments. "I'll buy that. No, I never did. I thought I did. I thought she was the most beautiful girl I've ever seen. She thought so too. It's a funny thing about love. You can't really love without being loved back. So I never loved her. She was incapable of love."

E. J. said, "The way you speak of her. It's . . . odd. As if she was dead."

It shook me for a moment. "As far as I'm concerned, she is."

Edith started to cry. It was a sound that did not differ very much from her whinnying social giggle. E. J. walked me out onto the porch.

"I don't know what to say," he said.

"I guess it's finished."

"I don't know what we did wrong. I don't know where it started. She always had everything she wanted. We tried to do everything for her and Eddie. I want her back, Jerry. I'm going to phone the police and give them the license number and description of the car. I want her back. What is the license number?"

"EX 93931," I said. He repeated it after me. It would be hard to read. It would take a skin diver with a good underwater light to read that license number.

"She's of age and it's her car," I said. "If she doesn't want to come back, the police can't make her. I don't know if they'll even look."

"She's a missing person, isn't she?"

"She sure is, E. J."

"Don't try to come to work tomorrow . . . today."

"You still want me working for you?"

"Why not, Jerry? Why not?"

"Say, I'd like to have that note she left me."

"Why?"

"I'd just like to have it. Okay?"

He nodded and went in and came out with the note. I put it in my pocket. We shook hands. It seemed a rather odd thing to do. His hand was small and soft, like a girl's.

"You didn't get your coffee," he said.

I could hear the endless sound of Edith crying. "That's okay."

I walked home. It was getting gray with the false dawn in the east. I didn't want to sleep in the room Lorraine and I had shared. I couldn't sleep in the bed where I had found her with Vince. The other guest room was not made up. I found sheets and made up the bed. I fell into sleep as though I had been beheaded.

When I woke up at noon it took me a few moments to figure out where I was, and then another ten seconds for all of the smashing weight of memory to fall upon me. I could not have done those things. I could not have killed her and buried her and killed Vince and sunk his body in Morning Lake. Not Jerome Durward Jamison. Not me. Not with these familiar hands. The hands looked just the same. In the bathroom mirror, the face looked just the same, except for the welts along my hairline left by the black flies.

Everything had seemed very clever and efficient and logical last night. Now I had the feeling that it was all full of holes, and people could look through the holes and see just what happened and why it happened. I could not think with any pleasure of the money under Camp Sootsus, or of the money down in the cellar. Plans were changed. I was going to have to find a new place for the money. A good place. And leave it there, untouched, for a long time . . . until it was accepted that Lorraine had run away with Vince and neither of them could be found. Then, and only then, could I think of going away.

I showered and shaved and put on a robe and went downstairs. Irene was sitting in the kitchen reading her Bible. She looked up and closed it and stood up.

"You'll be wanting breakfast now, Mr. Jamison?"

"Please, Irene. Mrs. Jamison isn't home."

"I saw her car gone."

"She won't be back, Irene. She's gone for good."

She thought that over and nodded her acceptance of it. "It's God's will," she said.

"And Mr. Biskay has gone too. They went away together."

She registered slight shock. Not very much. Her lips tightened. "She is the whore of Babylon, Mr. Jamison. I see more than folks intend me to see. But it's not my business to speak of it. It's been good to work for you. Will you be wanting me to stay on?"

"I don't know whether I'll try to keep up the house. Until I decide, if you could come in the morning and get my breakfast and clean the place up, that would be enough. I'll eat the other meals out."

She nodded and set about preparing my breakfast. The phone rang. She called to me and said it was Mrs. Pierson.

"Good morning, Mandy."

"My God, you certainly sound sour on such a handsome day! Did our little girl roll in too boiled to read the note you left? I gave up at midnight."

"I don't know what condition she was in. She came back while I was out. She packed her bags, left me a note and took off for good. With Vince. . . . Mandy?"

"I'm still here, darling. I'm trying to digest the entire morsel. Poor Jerry."

"And poor Lorraine."

"In a sense, yes."

"I don't want her back, Mandy. I've had it."

"And though she is one of my dearest friends, I must say she can be very naughty, and you've been more than patient. I give her about two weeks. And then she'll be back, very tragic and mysterious and contrite. And she will want to patch it all up."

"It won't work," I said. And I had a vision of her coming hop hop hop through the night in that tarp, with dirt clods falling from it, and I shuddered.

"She'll probably send me some gay mad postcard. Will you want to know where from?"

"Her people will. You can skip me."

"What are you going to do, darling? Sell the house and move into some grim little furnished room?"

"I don't think I can sell it without her signature. Maybe I can rent it. I don't know. I'll have to ask Archie Brill."

"He's quite good on divorce stuff, I hear. You could charge desertion, couldn't you? Or is adultery easier?"

"I don't know. I'll have to ask."

"Poor Lorraine. That friend of yours is certainly a yeasty item. Shall Tinker come comfort you in your loss, dear?"

"Now just a moment."

"I'm sorry. That wasn't in very good taste, was it? Darling, is this all over town already, or am I, for once, going to be the one to ride up and down the streets, clanging my little bell? You don't want it kept a secret, do you?"

"No. It doesn't matter."

"Then let us get off the line, pet, so I can get right back on. I shall spend the rest of the afternoon listening to assorted girlish squeals of shock."

My breakfast was ready. As Irene served it, I told her that Mrs. Jamison had left the bedroom in a mess and she might as well get it cleaned up. I asked her if she had seen the note I had left for Mrs. Jamison. She had thrown it away. She brought it to me, smoothing it out. I put it with Lorraine's green-ink note in the desk drawer in the living room.

I dressed and just as I was about to leave I remembered all the money I had folded and stuffed into the pockets of the hunting pants. It was a good thing I had remembered. The efficient Irene would have decided they should be cleaned, and she would have received a great shock when she emptied the pockets. I gathered all the bills together. Counted them. One hundred and nine-ty-nine hundred-dollar bills. Fifty had gone to the doctor. One had been burned. I remembered how we had laughed, Vince and I.

I was too concerned about getting out to Park Terrace to bother about a good place of concealment. I put two bills in my wallet and put the rest of the stack in the second drawer of my bureau, under a pile of clean sports shirts.

I parked on the job and walked up the line. They had finished pouring on two of the houses. They were pouring the third. The men were finishing off the slab on the second house. I looked at the raw wet cement that covered her grave. I wondered who would live in that house. And suddenly I wondered what would happen if it was never finished, if E. J. went broke. I had visions of another crew coming in. Another builder. Smaller lots. Smaller houses. "Break up that slab and move that fill out of there." And the dozer blade tilting the body out of the earth . . .

"Heard about your bad luck," Red Olin said. "Sorry, Jerry."

He startled me. He moved quietly for such a big man. "Thanks."

"I was remembering that first time we ever seen her."

"Over on Ridgemont Road."

"Sure is a pretty woman. Hard to figure women. Can't ever tell what they're thinking inside. Some of them just . . . take off. Never makes much sense."

"I guess it doesn't."

"You going to stay with the outfit?"

"For a while, I guess. I don't know."

"Think she'll come back, Jerry?"

"I don't know. I don't think I care much."

"I know how you feel. I know how I'd feel."

Then we talked about the job. Afterwards, I drove down to the office. E. J. and Eddie were out. Just Liz and the bookkeeper. I took her back to the familiar booth in the drugstore. She seemed subdued.

"It's . . . sort of simplified now, isn't it?" she said.

"It seems to be."

"She was no good, Jerry. Everybody knew that. No loyalty, Jerry. To you."

"I know."

"You act so strangely. You did say you . . . got what you went after on your trip."

"Yes, I did."

Her smile wasn't quite convincing. "When do I pack?"

"Not quite yet, Liz. I'll let you know."

She touched my hand. "We'll go away and it will be good, Jerry. It will be very good for both of us. We'll never look back. Never."

"As soon as we can."

When I went back to the house, it seemed very empty. Eight years form strong habits. Lorraine seemed to be just around every corner. I expected to hear the sound of her shower, and hear her "shower song"—"Frankie and Johnny" sung loudly. There were ghosts of her perfume in the silent air. Irene had tidied the bedroom.

I sat on my bed. I had a curious and vivid impression of the little copper-colored Porsche tooling west through the hot afternoon toward the mountains, with Lorraine at the wheel, her back hair snapping in the wind, teeth so white when she would turn and give Vince a quick bawdy smile. Their luggage was stacked behind them. The black tin suitcase was there. Vince lounged beside her, that indolent and arrogant half-smile on his brown face.

It seemed so vivid for a few moments that I thought it had to be real. Like puppets that come to life.

But the cement was hardening over her grave. And a curious fish was nosing the closed window of the Porsche.

I got out of the bedroom. There was too much of her still there.

I went down to the living-room desk and got out a sheet of paper and doodled aimlessly while I tried to devise a good place to put over three million six hundred thousand dollars in cash. A good safe place. A place I wouldn't have to worry about. And when I wanted to leave, I wanted to be able to get it in a hurry. It might remain hidden for six months or a year. It had to be safe from dampness and fire. It should be simple and easy, not involving a lot of work that might be noticed. The great bulk involved made the problem more difficult. I discarded the idea of renting large safety deposit boxes. I did not want to keep the money in the house, even sealed behind a partition.

If it could be handled casually, as though it were not money . . .

The idea began to take shape. I had to make a decision about the house. In anticipation of that decision, what could be more natural than to put a lot of my personal stuff in storage? A crate of books, say. A storage warehouse was a safe place. Get hold of a crate. Money in the bottom, perhaps wrapped in packages of three bricks each so as to look like books or records of some kind. When I was ready to go I could get the crate out of storage. Or even have it expressed from the warehouse to a new address. . . .

I heard the front doorbell. It was twenty minutes of five. The man on the front porch wore a tired tan suit, a white shirt with a frayed collar, a soiled panama hat pushed back to uncover a broad and placid forehead. He was stocky and his shoulders were enormous. His expression was one of patience and weariness and a kind of resignation. And he looked very familiar.

"Remember me, Jerry?"

"I . . . think I do. I'm sorry that I can't . . ."

"Nineteen forty. West Vernon High. Paul Heissen."

"My God, I'm sorry about being so stupid. Come on in." I hadn't known him well. In my last year at West Vernon High School, Paul Heissen, a sophomore, had become a first string center. We had certainly needed him. He was seventeen then, five feet eight, two hundred and five pounds. On defense they couldn't move him. I was defensive fullback, handling the linebacker slot behind the center of the line. Nobody made a nickel trying the center of our line all season long.

He came into the living room, filled a chair from arm to arm and dropped his hat on the floor.

"Can I get you a drink?"

"A beer if you've got one."

"Coming up."

"No glass. The can or the bottle is okay, Jerry."

I brought the two beers in. He took a long drink from the can, wiped his mouth on the back of his hand and belched. I had the idea from the look of him that he might be job-hunting.

"What can I do for you, Paul?"

"I guess you'd call this an official visit. E. J. Malton has been riding the chief all day about his missing daughter. So I got sent out to ask some damn fool questions."

"You're a cop?"

"Lieutenant Heissen. Overworked and underpaid. I was in the M.P.s in the war and I kind of drifted into it. I've seen you around town plenty of times, Jerry, but not to talk to."

"What do you want to know?"

He leaned sideways and pulled a dime notebook out of his pocket, clicked a ballpoint pen and turned to a clean page.

"She left last night. Know what time?"

"Sometime between ten and four in the morning. I think I got back around four. That's when I found the note. I went up and told E. J. I . . . I was pretty well loaded."

"Got the note?"

I got it from the desk and handed it to him. He copied the text of it into his notebook, chewing his lip as he did so. I handed him my note to her and said, "When I went out at ten I left this note for her." He copied it in the same stolid, methodical way.

"What threat?" he asked.

"She said she was going to leave me."

"You had a fight?"

"Yes." I decided that there was almost no likelihood of E. J. having told what I had told him about Lorraine and Vince. "A fight over our house guest. She . . .

seemed to be too friendly with him. They left together."

"How do you know they left together?"

"Paul, I don't know for sure. But when I came back they were both gone and so was her car and their luggage. He's very attractive to women. And Lorraine has been . . . restless lately."

"Restless?"

"Drinking too much. Playing around a little. Frankly, the marriage was going sour."

"No kids?"

"No."

"I've got four and another one on the way."

"It might have been different if there'd been kids. She had too much time on her hands."

"Now, how about this Biskay? How old?"

"About our age."

"Married?"

"No."

"What does he do for a living?"

"I'm not clear on the details, but I think he was working as an aide and pilot to some South American industrialist."

"Where did you meet him?"

"During the war. We were in the same O.S.S. unit. He was my c.o. He stopped by in April. He looked me up, stayed here a couple of nights. He said he had to have an operation. Something to do with his shoulder. About that time I quit my job. A disagreement with E. J. Malton. I took a trip, looking for a job. I looked in on Vince. He didn't have a very good setup. So I brought him back with me."

"Where did you find him?"

"In . . . in a borrowed apartment in Philadelphia."

"What was the address?"

"I can't remember. A street that had the name of a tree. Walnut or Chestnut or Maple. He told me that was where he'd be. He gave me the address when he was here in April."

"Because he knew you'd come and see him?"

"No. He had a proposition for me. I wasn't interested.

He told me if I changed my mind, I could write him there."

"What was the proposition?"

"Some work in South America. He was evasive about it. It didn't sound quite right. He's . . . a pretty wild type. I have a feeling he'd operate pretty close to the edge of the law. That isn't my style."

He asked for a description of Vince and I made it as complete as I could.

"Do you think he's got any kind of record?"

"I don't know."

"Well, his prints will be in the military files in Washington. I can get a cross check on them. If he's wanted, it'll be an excuse to have your wife stopped."

"I don't think she wants to be stopped."

"Her father wants her stopped. How about the car?" I described the car and gave him the license number. "Is it in her name?"

"Yes. The title is clear. She'd have the registration with her. She'd have no trouble selling it."

"Do you have any idea where they'd go?"

"I've no idea, Paul. I have a feeling . . . a hunch, that they'd leave the country. He didn't seem to be hurting for money. He'd probably head back for South America."

He frowned at his notebook. "Glad she's gone, Jerry?"

"In one way, yes. It was going sour. I want to get a divorce. In another sense, I miss her."

"Wife starts messing around with best friend. Sort of an old story, I guess. Lots of people get themselves shot that way."

"I'm not the violent type."

He grinned. "You sure as hell used to be."

"What will happen with this investigation, Paul?"

"I really don't know. It isn't illegal for a wife to take off. She didn't desert any kids. She didn't take your car. We can't put out a pickup order on her. But I can check out this Biskay and maybe we can find a reason to get him picked up. That would spoil her fun, I guess. And she might head on back home. Her daddy wants her back. But you don't?"

"No. I don't."

"You might change your mind."

"I don't think so."

"Where'd you find the note from her?"

"In the bedroom."

"Mind showing me?"

"Not at all." I took him upstairs. I propped the note against the dressing table mirror. It was a conspicuous place, readily noticeable when you walked into the room.

He looked around, walking slowly and heavily, whistling softly and expertly. "Nice place."

"Too big for just the two of us."

"What are you going to do? Keep on living here?"

"I guess so. For a little while, anyway."

He opened her closet door and said, "She left a lot of stuff."

"She took a lot of stuff too. She had a lot of stuff. She bought clothes by the bale."

"Where was Biskay? What room?"

I showed him. "What shape was he in? Get around all right?"

"Arm in a sling and a bad limp," I said. "But he could get around."

"What was the limp from?"

"They operated on his hip too, I think."

"Don't you know?"

"Paul, you're sounding like a cop. Vince wasn't the sort of guy who told you very much about his problems."

"A guy takes him in and he takes off with the guy's wife. Must be pure son of a bitch."

"I didn't think he'd do a thing like that."

"Some people just don't give a damn, I guess."

"That's the way Vince is."

We went back downstairs and he went over and picked up his hat, grunting as he did so. He said, "Mr. Malton gave us some good shots of her. If there's something we can use on Biskay, it won't be any trick finding a car that conspicuous. Or a woman that conspicuous. I saw her a couple of times. Didn't know who she was until I saw the pictures. She looks like that movie woman, Elizabeth Taylor."

"People have always told her that. She liked being told that."

"Nice to see you again, Jerry. Maybe we can have a beer together some time."

"I'd like that, Paul."

"They never did get that nose set all the way straight, did they?"

"That was the Proctor game."

"I remember that big fullback they had. He was hard to stop, that boy was. Well, be seeing you."

He went out and got into a sedan at the curb, waved as he started up. When I exhaled I felt as if I was getting rid of stale air I had been retaining for an hour. It was going to be all right. There wasn't going to be any problem. It had been awkward trying to lie about Philadelphia, but I didn't think he had suspected anything. And he'd left the note from Lorraine behind. He had copied it. I thought again about how they could determine the age of handwriting. I took both notes and tore them up and flushed them down the drain.

And the moment they were both gone it occurred to me that it hadn't been proven that the note was in her handwriting.

Chapter 10

I arrived at Camp Sootsus at dusk the same evening of Paul Heissen's visit to the house. I retrieved the black tin suitcase and put it in the wagon and got out of there. I hid it in the cellar under the wood, after replacing the bundles that had been my share. I liked looking at it all back together again. All in the same place. A dizzying, overpowering amount of tightly packed bills. It made my breath shallow to look at it.

108

On Friday morning I went to Park Terrace and told Red there was some stuff I wanted to put in storage. I told him the dimensions of the crate I wanted. I told him I wanted it sturdy. He put a carpenter on it. By the time I had finished the usual check of progress on the job, the man had finished it and put it in the station wagon. It was made of scrap half-inch plywood braced with one-by-twos and screwed together. On the way home I stopped and bought twine and heavy brown wrapping paper.

Irene had left for the day by the time I got home. I made certain the doors were locked. I wrapped the bricks of tightly wired money, four bricks in a package, side by side. Seventeen brown packages. There was two hundred thousand dollars in each package except the last one. The brick of five hundreds went in that one, so there was four hundred thousand in the last one. I packed them into the crate. It nearly filled it. I wrestled it up the cellar stairs and into the living room. I filled the crate the rest of the way with books, my books from the living-room shelves. I fitted the lid on, screwed it down, wrote my name on the plywood top with a red crayon.

I found a storage warehouse in the yellow pages and phoned. They said they would take a single crate. I told them it was heavy. The truck arrived within the hour. Two men carried it out and drove away with it. The warehouse receipt was on flimsy orange paper and it had a lot of fine print on the back. I read every word of it. I had automatic insurance of five dollars per cubic foot. The crate was two by two by three. Sixty dollars insurance. In case of loss.

I needed a good place to put the receipt. I roamed through the house until I found the right place. Lorraine had decided one time that she would like to learn how to play the recorder. So she had bought herself a very fine one, and an instruction book. She had made mournful hooting sounds around the house for about ten days before giving up for good. I took the leather case from the closet shelf, untwisted the mouthpiece, rolled the receipt into a tube and inserted it and put the mouthpiece back on and put the recorder back on the shelf.

Then I sat down in the living room, legs outstretched, ankles crossed. I went over the whole thing. As near as I could tell, it was clean. There was nothing to do but wait it out.

I became aware of Lorraine looking at me. I looked at her across the living room and then got up and went over and picked up the picture in its frame of hammered silver. It was a black and white picture, taken in Bermuda. During our honeymoon. She wore white shorts and a black sweater. She stood smiling into the camera, holding the handlebars of an English bike, looking ready to swing onto it and pedal away. I remembered how it had been in Bermuda.

I looked at her face in the picture and all of a sudden I felt ill. I felt as though I stood on a high place, with nothing under me but a terrible emptiness. I put the picture down. She didn't stop watching me. I moved over to the side and she was still watching me, and smiling. It was an odd smile. As though she knew something I didn't. As though she remembered something I had forgotten.

The black tin suitcase! Thank you, Lorraine. I got it out of the cellar. I stomped the catches with my heel until they were ruined. I drove to the city dump and when I was certain I was not observed, I threw it over the crest of a mountain of trash.

Saturday was an interminable and boring day. I got quietly tight all by myself on Saturday night and went to bed early, so early that when I awakened at eight on Sunday morning I had slept through any possibility of hangover. I put on slacks and a sports shirt, made my breakfast, and made the Sunday paper last a long time.

The day ahead seemed as empty and endless as Saturday had been. I had resented the meaningless activities of most of my Sundays with Lorraine, but at least there had been something going on. At eleven I went out and did some aimless work in the yard.

I was clipping the hedge and just beginning to work up a sweat when Tinker Velbiss appeared on the other side of the hedge. She wore a green and white striped blouse with a demure collar, knee-length tailored green shorts. Her hair was orange flame in the sun. Her nose was peeling from recent sunburn, and she seemed to have a great many more freckles than usual. She stood hipshot, smiling at me, a very saucy look in her eyes.

"Don't you have enough muscles?" she asked.

"Good morning."

"I had to come and see you. Sort of an anniversary, isn't it?"

I looked at her blankly. "Anniversary?"

"Last Sunday, stupid! Or were you too crocked to remember? How desperately flattering!"

"I remember distinctly."

"Oh, thank you, thank you." Last Sunday was an eon back. Last Sunday was something that had happened to a Jerry Jamison I could barely remember.

"You didn't waste any time running to Mandy Pierson with a play by play, Tink."

She gave me a look of forced and solemn innocence. "I never did."

"Mandy seemed to have the score."

She walked around onto my side of the hedge and said, "You're angry, aren't you? Well, maybe I did give her sort of a little bit of a hint. You must think I was perfectly bold and awful last Sunday. I was just reckless and a little drunky and so damn terribly tired of Charlie. But you see, Charlie reaped all the benefits. Well, almost all. I've been a perfect lamb to him all week. A lot happens in a week, doesn't it, sweet? Any picture postcards from Lorraine?"

"Not yet."

"You look all hot and sticky. Why don't you ask me to sit in the shade and have a drink? Where's your lawn furniture?"

"I didn't get around to telling Irene to have somebody

bring it up out of the cellar. But you can have a drink. Where's Charlie?"

"Oh, he's having a big boyish day for himself. He's at the club. It's some kind of a tournament thing. You know he can't ever win anything because he turns in low scores so he can admire the nice low handicap they post for him in the pro shop. Then in a tournament he has to grovel around saying he's off his game. He's out there hacking and slicing away, gay as a lark. It lasts way into the evening and then they have a big beer thing. I dumped my little monsters with Charlie's mother. I have to pick them up at seven tonight. So I thought I would use some of this big broad day over here with you going cluck cluck about Lorraine. Are you still terribly annoyed at me?"

"No. Of course not."

We went into the kitchen and it seemed very dim in there after the bright hot sunshine.

"Something tall and ginny," she said. "Do we have tonic? Good. I'll break out the ice, dear."

"Why the hell did you inform Mandy, Tink?"

"Oh, we're very good friends, sort of. Anyway, we've got the goods on each other. A sort of enforced trust you might say. Anyhow, I didn't come right out. I just hinted a little bit."

"Did you and Lorraine play the same little game?"

"Glory, no! Lorraine gets too potted. She might let something slip in front of Charlie."

I poured gin into the first glass. As I was about to stop she reached over and held the neck of the bottle down with one finger until the glass was half full. "That's mine," she said. "I don't like the taste of tonic."

When the two drinks were ready we clinked glasses and sipped. She cocked her head on one side and said, "Glory, you've got to stop being all funny and shy with me, Jerry. It makes me feel slutty." She put her glass on the counter, took mine out of my hand and put it aside, then came into my arms, fitting the warm length of her-self adeptly against me, kissing me with a heady and lusty abandon.

"There now," she said, and picked up her drink. "Let's be friends."

"We're friends."

"Good friends?"

"Yep."

"Expecting any company?"

"No, why?"

"Let's go on a picnic, darling."

"Picnic?"

"Of course. Everybody goes on Sunday picnics. Where's the red plastic thing you people have that keeps ice cubes cold?" I found it for her. "Now we lay in a stock of ice. And that's a nearly new bottle of gin. Let me see. We have glasses. Cigarettes. Five bottles of tonic. Hmm. You will go on a picnic, won't you?"

"All right."

"Now you go around like a dear and make sure the doors are locked."

I stared at her. "Where do we have this picnic, Tinker?"

"Upstairs, darling, of course! Aren't you being a little bit dull today? I come over offering solace and comfort and picnics and things and you just give me that buggy-eyed boggle. Come along, dear. These are really the best picnics. No ants."

After the long interlude of casual sexual abandon with Tinker, I lay on my bed with a new drink within reach, cigarette in hand, ash tray cool on my chest and felt drab, hopeless and depressed. I could hear her paddling about, jingling the hangers in Lorraine's closet, opening drawers, going through Lorraine's things. I wished she would stop. I wished she would put on her green shorts and her striped blouse and go away, but I felt too listless to tell her to.

I felt very queer about myself. It seemed to me that I had shut away all real awareness of what I had done, closed it up in a corner of my mind and nailed the door shut. But in the depression that invariably follows a loveless conjoining, the secret door had sagged open and

I had to take an unwilling look at the deeds, and the implications of the deeds.

It hadn't been what I had wanted to happen to me. This wasn't the life I had wanted to have. I was supposed to be one of the good guys. Jerry Jamison. I'd been brought up thinking of myself as one of the good guys. If you were the other kind you eventually got shot down, you spun and fell dramatically in the cowtown dust, or they clanged the big doors shut behind you, big doors in a gray wall.

I had to pick the words up one at a time, hold them gingerly with the fingers of my mind, turn them this way and that and look at them curiously. Murderer. Thief.

It couldn't be me. I went back over the chain of events trying to see where I could have broken the pattern. I wanted to be able to tell myself that once it had begun, I had been swept along with it, powerless to change any of it. But I could see a dozen ways and times I could have broken free of it. One bleak fact kept intruding itself. I kept remembering the look of the money when I had opened that black suitcase. And I had known when I had first looked at it that it was all going to be mine. Somehow.

So what the hell was wrong with me? Had I been just an artificial good guy, who had lacked the motivation to turn him into a bad guy? Or had the eight years with Lorraine changed me? Or just the feeling of being in a trap I couldn't get out of.

But it had been done. Lorraine and Vince were gone for good. And no matter where I was, there would never be one day free of fear. Or free of memory. Or free of this feeling of sickness inside.

Tinker said, "Honey, she must have really left in a rush."

"What do you mean?"

"She only bought this last week. I was with her. I think it's pretty dreamy. It cost forty-nine fifty. It's the softest cashmere I ever felt."

I raised my head and looked at her. She had put the soft gray sweater on. A sweater on a naked woman is a singularly unappealing garment. And Tinker had recently had a touch of sun. Her long plump legs were pink, and from the tops of her thighs to the edge of the gray sweater she was red-head white.

"She forgot it, I guess."

"I don't see how she could have." Tinker turned away from the mirror. "Upstairs we're about the same, but I'm hippier. Honey, why can't I sort of borrow this? It's a good color for me. If she comes back, she won't mind. And if she doesn't, it will be a sort of keepsake."

"I don't give a damn what you do."

"Thank you, darling. You're so tender and sweet."

I sat up and took a long pull on my drink. Tinker had made it. It was mostly raw gin. I felt it hit and radiate. I wanted a lot of gin. I wanted enough so it would stop the big wheel that kept going around in my head. The wheel had vivid pictures all around the rim of it. Pictures of Vince and Lorraine and the money.

She wheedled another sweater, a pleated skirt, a handful of costume jewelry, two pair of shoes and a pair of sandals. Her feet were the same size as Lorraine's, just a shade wider. Then she felt hungry. She put on a yellow robe of Lorraine's and went downstairs, scrambled some eggs and fixed bacon and brought two plates up. We ate and we had another drink, and she came back to bed. We were both getting quite thoroughly plotzed.

When I was awakened by the front doorbell I looked at my watch and saw that it was a little after five. Tinker was curled against me, humid in sleep. I pushed her away and she mumbled a complaint. I heard the doorbell again. I felt like I had an icepick socketed in each temple, and a mouth like a bus station ashtray. But the gin was still at work. I felt tall and wobbly on my legs, and remote from reality. I looked at Tinker. She slept with her mouth open and there were two pimples on her left shoulder.

I found my robe and put it on, combed my hair back with my fingers and went down the stairs. The doorbell rang again.

It was Liz Addams. She was very agitated. She came into the hallway and said, "Oh, I'm so glad you're home, Jerry. Are you all right? You look so strange."

"Just woke up. I'm a little fuzzy."

"And a little drunk?"

"Maybe. Just a little."

"Jerry, two men have been questioning me. Asking all sorts of odd things about you. I don't know what it's all about, but it seemed so strange. They're from some kind of Washington agency I never heard of before. I thought you should know about it and . . ."

I was standing with my back to the stairway. She looked over my shoulder. She stopped talking. Her eyes widened, and then suddenly her face went quite still and dead. Something went out of her eyes, something I had needed, and even before I turned, I knew that I would never see that particular light in her eyes again.

Tinker had come down, barefoot, to within four steps of the bottom of the stairs and stood in plain sight. She had put Lorraine's robe over her shoulders, sleeves dangling, and she was holding it together in front. Her red hair was tousled, her face blurred and puffed with sleep, her lips swollen. She was so very obviously a woman who had just gotten out of bed.

"Oh!" she said in a small voice. "I thought it was Mandy. Mandy Pierson. I mean your voices sound alike. I'm so terribly sorry, really."

She turned around and stumbled. She went down onto her hands and knees on the stairs and lost the robe. As she snatched it up and put it around herself again, she gave us a wide muzzy smile and said, "Woops!" and plodded back up out of sight.

Liz did not look at me again. She turned and opened the door. There wasn't a damn thing I could say. Nothing at all. I watched her through the screen as she walked down the porch steps and out of my life.

I closed the door and went back upstairs. Tinker sat on the dressing table bench, wearing the yellow robe properly, combing her harsh and vivid hair. She looked at me meekly in the mirror and said, "I guess I goofed, huh?"

"You goofed."

"That was the blondie from the office. The one you've had a thing about."

"That's right."

"She didn't look like she was ready to be very broad-minded."

"No."

"I'm sorry if I spoiled anything."

"Just tell me one thing, Tink. If you really thought it was Mandy, why the hell would you come down?"

"Oh, I guess it seemed like a good idea. I mean like a joke. And there's some of Lorraine's things that won't fit me that would fit her. She's slim in the hips like Lorraine. Anyway, Mandy wouldn't tell anybody. She's real fun. You'd like her lots. We don't have any secrets from each other."

"I guess you don't."

"Mandy really likes you. I think she'd like to come and have a little visit with you, dear."

"What the hell are you trying to do? Bribe me with Mandy? I don't understand you people."

She turned around and gave me a look of mock solemnity. "Glory, you poor old beast. You're all tied up in knots, aren't you? Sweetie, it's like Charlie keeps saying. We all have measurable amounts of Strontium 90 in our bones. Did you know that? It's very creepy when you think about it. So the way you go about not thinking of it is by having fun. And when you're having fun you only think about the fun. Mandy and I are very careful, darling, but we still have slightly horrible reputations. But it doesn't bother us any more than it does Lorraine. Darn it, I feel so sticky. Can I use your shower? Did Lorraine leave a bathing cap around?"

"Bathroom closet, top shelf."

"Thanks, sweetie." She shed the robe and padded into the bathroom. In a moment the shower began. I went down to the kitchen and made coffee, hot and black. I couldn't stop thinking of the look on Liz's face. And wondering about the two men from Washington.

I had poured the second cup, still too hot to drink, when Tink came down. The blurred look was gone. She looked brisk and alert. She carried her loot wrapped in the pleated skirt.

"Darling, I'd stay and swab up glasses and plates and things, but I've really got to run. Do you mind?"

"Run along. Please do."

"Don't be so grim, baby. I'm sorry I messed up your little office romance. Brother, I really did it, didn't I?"

"You did it."

She came over to where I was sitting, ran her fingers through my hair and kissed the corner of my eye. "You're very pleasurable, my lamb, and don't glower about that plain-looking blonde. We'll have lots and lots of cozy fun, and we'll make Jerry forget all about her, won't we?"

She went out the back way. I tried the coffee. It was still too hot. I carried it upstairs. I wanted to take a shower. The bathroom appalled me. It was awash. She had apparently floundered around like a damn sea lion. It was sticky-hot, perfumed, humid and thoroughly steamed. I opened the window wide, used a towel to sop up the water on the floor.

I took a shower, drank my coffee, made the bed, cleaned up the litter, took three aspirin, put on a fresh sports shirt and slacks. I inspected the end result. My eyes had a hollow look.

Just as I reached the foot of the stairs the doorbell rang again. I had the crazy and ridiculous hope that Liz had come back.

But it was Lieutenant Paul Heissen, as wide and stolid and placid as before, but with a look of a man in an uncomfortable situation.

"Come on in, Paul. Beer?"

"Not this time, thanks."

He took the same chair as before, dropped his hat in the same place. "This is one of the things you got to do when you're a cop, Jerry. I might as well level with you. Old lady Malton can't figure her darling daughter taking off without a word to her. And she finally got E. J. Malton all worked up about it. They paid the chief a call yesterday and I was called in on it. They say you weren't getting along very good. It took a long time before they came right out with it, but they finally said it. They think it's possible you killed her and that Biskay."

"That's a pretty weird idea."

"Probably is. But I have to check it out. That's what I've been doing. I know you've got the answers, but I have to bother you so I can write a complete report on it. The lady across the street, Mrs. Hinkley, says she saw your wife drive in about one o'clock last Wednesday. I can't find anybody who saw her after that. You came home in the middle of the afternoon and ran out of gas. I checked that out with Mrs. Sittersall."

"Who? Oh, Irene. Yes."

"You met her when she was coming to work and told her your wife wasn't well. Why did you do that?"

I heaved a deep sigh. I told him that I was trying to save some of Lorraine's reputation when I hadn't told him all the facts before. I described how I had come home and how I had found them.

"A lot of people have turned up dead when that happens."

"I know. But I wasn't in the mood to kill anybody. He wasn't in good shape. And I . . . I've had reason to suspect her in the past. This was the first time I had proof. She locked herself in the bedroom. I took gas down to get the car going and ran into Irene and I didn't think it was a very good situation for her to walk in on. I mean it was pretty tense around here."

"So you drove her to a bus stop and got the car gassed up. Then what?"

"I came back here. I had a couple of drinks and then I took off. I was trying to think things out. I just drove around."

"When did you get back?"

"I don't really know. It was dark. Vince was asleep. Lorraine was gone, but her car was in the garage."

"I checked with Amanda Pierson. She stopped by at

about nine-thirty. How long had you been home?"

"Maybe fifteen minutes. Twenty minutes." I knew Mandy had stopped by much earlier than nine-thirty. Her error might come in handy.

"Where do you think your wife was?"

"I don't know. She visits around the neighborhood a lot. Maybe she was just walking. She does that sometimes. Or maybe, hell, she was hiding somewhere in the house. I would never have thought to look for her."

"What did you do?"

"After Mandy phoned I went out again, leaving a note for Lorraine. You saw the note. I had more drinks and went out. I know I stopped at the Hotel Vernon bar. Timmy should remember. You can understand why I was a pretty mixed-up guy. I stopped at a couple of other joints too. Frankly, Paul, I was in no shape to be driving. I could have killed somebody. Or myself. I didn't want to go back home. I even drove up to Morning Lake. The Maltons have a camp up there. We use it. I thought I'd stay up there. But the black flies were too fierce."

"That's where you got those bites, then?"

"That's right. So I came back thinking I'd have it out with her. I'd come full circle back to thinking that maybe we could still make a go of it. But they were gone. And her car. I could see she'd packed in a hell of a hurry."

"Mrs. Sittersall told me about that."

"I read the note and took it down the road to E. J.'s place and made a fool of myself."

He looked over the notes he had written. "Now here's something you can clear up. Mrs. Sittersall didn't see any scratches on your face. But you say you didn't see your wife again."

"She gouged me right after I found them, before she locked herself in. I tried to cover them up. I did a fair job, using some of Lorraine's pancake makeup. Irene isn't very observant."

"What gas station did you go to?" I told him, realizing uncomfortably that this was a thorough, plodding, methodical man. He would check there.

"Now then, Jerry," he said. "On Friday a truck came here and two men carried out a heavy packing case and drove away with it. That information was volunteered by Mrs. Hinkley. What was in it?"

I gestured at the book shelves. "Books and personal papers. I'm going to get around to putting the rest of my personal stuff in storage too. I was just making a start. I'm not going to keep on living here, Paul. Hell, one man in a house this size!"

"Got the warehouse receipt?"

"Of course."

"I'd like to see it, Jerry. Sorry to be such a damn nuisance."

I could get it but he would see me get it, and it would be awkward to try to explain the weird hiding place.

"Give me a minute to think where I put it. I've been pretty mixed up the last few days."

"Take your time. In the meantime, I'd like to have that note she left."

I'd been afraid of that. "I'm sorry, Paul, but I threw that out. I threw both notes out. Hell, you took down what they said."

"The Maltons aren't certain the note was in their daughter's handwriting."

"But it *was!*"

"If it's gone, it makes it sort of tough to prove."

"I don't see what the hell difference it makes. Lorraine will tell you she wrote it."

"It would just make it easier if you still had it, Jerry. That's all."

I went over to the desk and opened the drawer and made a pretense of hunting for the warehouse receipt.

He stood up and said, "Mind if I look around a little?"

"What for?"

"Just so I can put in my report that I looked the house over. That's expected. I'd have to do it even if I had to get a warrant, Jerry."

"Why don't you book me for murder?"

"Don't get nasty. Let's do this the easy way. Hell, I

121

don't think you killed her. But what I think doesn't matter. I just investigate, like I'm told to do."

"Okay. Go look around. I'll hunt for the receipt."

He went out into the kitchen and I heard him go down the cellar stairs. For one cold moment I couldn't remember whether any of the money was still there. My mind wasn't working well. It had been misted by gin and by an excess of Tinker. I took the receipt from its hiding place, straightened it out and waited until I heard Paul coming back up into the kitchen. I took it to him. He looked at it, nodded, pocketed it.

"Tomorrow morning we'll go take a look at the crate."

"Why, for God's sake?"

"Because if we don't, I get asked why we didn't and then do I say it was too much trouble?"

"Okay, okay. So we look at the crate. We'll take every stinking book out of it and read every page."

"I'm trying to make this easy, Jerry."

"I'm sorry, Paul. I know that. I'm just edgy. I guess I'm upset about throwing her note away."

"Would it still be in the trash, maybe?"

"No. I tore it up and threw it out the car window."

"Too bad."

"But it can't be critically important, can it?"

"No. I wouldn't say that."

He was frighteningly thorough. He asked a hell of a lot of questions. He picked up the comb from Lorraine's dressing table, and pulled a tuft of crisp red hair out of the teeth and looked at me.

"A . . . a friend of Lorraine's. Mrs. Velbiss. Tinker Velbiss. Lorraine had borrowed something of hers and didn't return it before she left, so when Tinker came over I told her to come on up and get it."

"So she combed her hair."

"Okay, Paul, damn it. She came over to talk about Lorraine, and it ended up in a way we hadn't planned. I guess I'm . . . vulnerable."

"Jerry, look. Don't lie to me. Not in little things. Not in anything. Don't lie to me. That's important."

"Okay, Paul. It won't happen again."

122

"I was going to ask you about Mrs. Addams in the office. I heard a rumor you've been friendly. A thing like that could be considered a motive."

"She's a splendid person. I like her. But that's all there is. I wish I'd married her instead of Lorraine. But I didn't."

He made me make a list, from memory, of the things Lorraine had taken with her. He looked the station wagon over carefully. He checked the garden tools. He thumbed dirt off the shovel I had buried her with and crumbled it between his fingers. I watched him, trying to breathe normally. He asked no questions.

It was well after dark when he finally left. He said he would meet me at the warehouse at nine in the morning.

He apologized again for having to bother me. I said it was all right. I apologized for being irritable.

Chapter 11

Paul Heissen was waiting for me when I got to the warehouse at nine o'clock. I had brought a screwdriver along. They made a fuss about the trouble this was causing them and quieted down when Heissen said he was from the police.

I unscrewed the lid. Paul lifted out books. He uncovered the brown paper packages.

"Old records," I said. "Business papers. House plans. Architectural magazines. Stuff like that. Want me to open one?"

He prodded a package with a thick thumb. "No need of that."

We fitted the books back in. I screwed the lid on. He thanked the warehouse man and we walked out. He walked to my car with me and said, "That bartender at the Hotel Vernon said you were in around ten o'clock and pretty well loaded."

"I guess I was."

"If you'd ordered a second drink you wouldn't have gotten it. He said you were complaining about wife trouble."

"That's what I had."

"I guess you did."

"What happens now, Paul?"

"We wait and see if we can get a line on the car. Now she's missing under suspicious circumstances. We can put it on the tape. We have already. Nationwide. But quiet like. It won't alert any nosy newspaper people. You don't have to worry about that."

"And if you don't find her in a hurry?"

"I'd say if we don't find her in two weeks, then we'll have to go through this whole thing again. Bring you in and get a complete and detailed statement."

"You people could keep bothering me forever."

"Not forever, Jerry. Just until we find out what happened to her."

"Oh."

I started the car motor. He started away and then turned back and leaned on my window and said, "Say, a funny thing about this Biskay."

"What is that?"

"Usually they're fast down there. They check the military prints against the central FBI files and give us a fast no or a fast yes with details. This time it sounds like they're stalling. I never had that happen before. Maybe it ties in with there being strangers in town."

"Strangers?"

"I don't know much about them. They checked in as a matter of courtesy. They could be Treasury people. It would look like maybe Washington is interested in this Biskay. That's just a guess. They been to see you yet?"

"Not yet."

I drove to the office. Liz was at her desk. She looked at me with complete and perfect indifference. For a time I had been a part of her life. But all that had been very quickly canceled out by a redheaded slut on a staircase. A suburban type, country-club, gin-fed, plump-legged, mischievous, meaningless slut—as exclusive as a roller towel, as standardized as beanwagon coffee, as significant as a handshake.

It seemed such a hell of a waste.

But I was becoming a specialist in waste these days. Of myself and everybody else. But there was still the money, wasn't there? And a glorious golden future. No sweat. No strain.

I asked Liz if E. J. was in.

She got up and went to the door to his office, tapped on it, opened it halfway and spoke to him in a low voice.

"Jerry?" he bellowed to me. "Come on in, come on in."

She held the door all the way open for me. I passed close to her. Close enough to catch the fragrance of her. And close enough to sense how she shrank away from me without actually moving. The way she would avert her eyes from a nuisance on the sidewalk. She closed the door behind me.

"E. J.," I said, sitting down at his gesture of invitation, "the police are prying around because it seems you and Edith have some crazy idea I killed Lorraine."

It was more blunt than he had anticipated, I am sure. His face turned red quite quickly. "We . . . uh . . . Edith and I, asked that every possibility be investigated, Jerry. If they seem to be excessively diligent . . ."

"Come off it, E. J."

"Our children have always been very close to us, Jerry. I mean it has been a good relationship. Even if Lorraine did run off with your . . . friend, Edith seems to think she would let us know, somehow."

"*If* she ran off? What else happened to her, E. J.?"

"That's what the police are investigating."

"So where do I fit? It makes it pretty damn awkward trying to work for you. It makes it a hell of a situation."

He looked down at his neat little pink and white hands and folded them together atop the green desk blotter, and they massaged each other tenderly.

"I really think, Jerry, it would be best if you took a leave of absence until . . . this is all settled."

The door opened behind me and Eddie came striding in. He stood over me, feet planted, face working. I don't know who he was imitating. Kirk Douglas or Burt Lancaster. He didn't do it very well. He was as awesome as Bugs Bunny.

"What have you done with my sister, Jamison?" he snarled.

I stared at him, and then I yawned at him.

He stamped his foot. It is a gesture no adult male can get away with. "I asked you a question!" he said, but his voice was half an octave higher and he was trembling.

"Go crumple your hanky," I said. He swung at me with a wild roundhouse right. I snapped my head back and felt the breeze of it across my lips. The miss spun him off balance so that he sat on my lap. I pushed him up and away. He yelped something that I couldn't understand and went storming out, slamming the door behind him. I looked at E. J. He looked shamed and apologetic.

"Eddie is very upset," he said.

"So am I."

"They were very close," he said.

"Past tense?" I asked.

He pinched a trout lip and pulled on it and let go. "I keep doing that," he said. "Edith becomes hysterical when I do it. I do it without thinking. It's a kind of instinct, I guess. Something tells me she's dead. And logic doesn't do any good. Last night I dreamed about her and she was dead."

"I'll bet she's dead," I said. "Dead drunk. She's probably baking it out beside a swimming pool out in Palm Springs." I got up. "Okay, I'll take a leave of absence. With pay."

"With pay, Jerry. No hard feelings."

"There are hard feelings. But before it becomes official I'll go out on the job and wind up a couple of details. With your permission."

"Of course, of course."

I left him sitting there. I did not glance toward Liz Addams as I left. There was no break or hesitation in the rippling staccato of her typing. It followed me until the street door closed behind me and cut it off.

I sat behind the wheel of the wagon for a few minutes before starting it up. In E. J.'s office I had been big and brave and bold. But I'd left a trail of sawdust all the way to the car. I felt meager and shrunken. I didn't like him dreaming she was dead. I had not dreamed at all since . . . it had happened. I hoped I wouldn't. I didn't want to do any more dreaming, not so long as I lived. I felt that should I dream they'd both come after me. Vince and Lorraine. And I might not wake up.

It seemed a very bad thing that E. J. had dreamed her dead. When Irene had served me my breakfast, she had told me about all the questions the man asked her. I remembered Paul Heissen's thick thumb prodding the baled money. I remembered the long tumbling sound of Vince's fall, with three leaden pellets in his head. I remembered that the hole was too narrow for her, that she lay on her side in the bottom of it. She always slept the best on her side, but not cold and straight in a tarp—curled and warm and tousled, with the high mound of hip that dipped down into the indentation of her slim waist, and then the long straight line from waist to shoulder. But they didn't bury people the way they liked to sleep. There had been air trapped in the Porsche. A little air. Probably enough to turn it again under water so that it would be resting on its wheels. So that Vince slept sitting up. In the water.

I shook myself like a weary horse in fly season and turned the ignition key and drove out to the job.

I was nearly through explaining to Red Olin what I wanted done when they showed up. They got me aside. There were two of them. They drove a rental sedan, a red and white thing with towering tail fins like a rocket to Mars. They looked like Yankees during the off season, when ballplayers sell bonds and insurance and real estate. They were neatly and carefully dressed, and they had that curious air of courtesy plus arrogance that you would expect from any Yankee on or off the diamond. The big brown-haired one with all the shoulders was named Barnstock. He would be an outfielder, a power hitter. Give him a reasonable piece of the ball and he'd hammer it out of the park, even hitting to the wrong field. Quellan, the other one, black-haired, limber, rangy—six three, with big knobby hands—was obviously a pitcher. When he was right he would whistle them in. Nobody would dig in and get comfortable batting because of that tendency towards wildness.

I asked to see identification and Quellan showed me his. I said I had never heard of the agency. "We don't spend a dime on public relations," Barnstock said.

I asked for another fifteen minutes on the job, and then they could have me for the rest of the day, if they wanted that much time. They waited.

Barnstock rode with me in the wagon. I followed the big tail fins. We put both cars in the lot across from the side entrance to the Hotel Vernon. We said it was a hot day, and it looked like a long hot summer, but of course that was what you had to expect in this neck of the woods. Long hot summers. They had a small suite on the eighth floor. We got all comfy in the sitting room. Barnstock broke out the tape recorder, put a big new reel on, set a table mike in the middle of the coffee table. I sat on the couch. Quellan sat beside me with a stenographer's notebook open on his knee, a fat green pen in hand. Barnstock pulled a chair over so that he sat on the other side of the coffee table, facing me.

"Mr. Jamison," Quellan said, "this is not a formal interrogation. It may take quite a long time. Tape is better than notes or memory. I hope you have no objection to our recording what you say?"

"Not at all."

Quellan nodded at Barnstock. He started the tape up, counted to ten slowly, reversed the tape, played his voice back over the monitor speaker, erased the count, reset the tape and said, "Monday, May nineteen, eleven-twenty a.m. Interrogation by Quellan and Barnstock of Jerome Jamison in the matter of Vincente Biskay."

Quellan took the first question. "Mr. Jamison, in your

own words I would like you to tell me the circumstances of your first meeting with Mr. Biskay. Be as thorough as possible. When we want anything clarified, we will interrupt you and ask additional questions."

It was certainly thorough. They took me through the entire period from when I had first reported to Vince at Galle to when I last saw him from the airplane window in Calcutta. Their questioning was polite but thorough. Under the continual pressure I was able to remember names and incidents that I had thought completely forgotten. At one o'clock we took a break and had lunch brought up to the suite. I was down to my last cigarette, and Barnstock, on the phone, ordered up two more packs along with the sandwiches and coffee. The chill and hum of the air-conditioning made the suite a small private world.

During the half-hour break while the recorder was turned off, we talked baseball and bass fishing. I felt at ease. There was nothing ominous about them. I had nothing to hide that had transpired during the period we were covering. Their official curiosity about Vince seemed curiously compulsive. Habits, tastes, fragments of background.

By quarter after two we had covered the war part of it.

"When did you next see Biskay?" Quellan asked.

"Last month."

Barnstock interrupted, saying, "Ed, I think we can save a little time here by telling Mr. Jamison that we know that Biskay arrived at the Vernon Airport at ten minutes of five on Friday, April twenty-fifth, on American flight 712 out of Chicago. He had entered the country on an Eastern flight from Mexico City to New Orleans. He was using a forged passport which identified him as a Paraguayan national named Miguel Brockman. He left Vernon Airport at one-fifteen on American flight 228 to Chicago, made connections there to New Orleans and picked up his reservation on Eastern to Mexico City."

Barnstock had not referred to any notes. All the information had been memorized. It made me distinctly uneasy.

"Fine," Quellan said. "We know from tracing his movements that Biskay came to this country for the sole purpose of visiting you, Mr. Jamison. Did you have prior knowledge of this visit?"

"No."

"Then we can pick up the thread again at the time he appeared. What time did he arrive at your home, and who answered the door?"

I opened my mouth and closed it again. I could see just how carefully and thoroughly I had been mousetrapped. Up until that point I had made a great effort to be completely frank and honest with them. Why not? All that war stuff couldn't do me any harm. But for a long time I had been very detailed and explicit, and I could not show a shift of attitude, a sudden reticence. And I knew that my powers of invention were not adequate to the job. I could not continue with the exhaustive detail, even though this last meeting with him was much clearer in my mind.

They talk about trap questions. This was not a trap question, but a trap situation. They both looked at me. The silence grew longer. The big reel on the tape recorder turned, recording the silence. They looked at each other. Barnstock reached out and turned the recorder off. Quellan took one of my cigarettes and lighted it.

"Jamison, we're not interested in any criminal prosecution. We're not interested in accumulating facts that might lead to a criminal prosecution by some other legal agency." I did not fail to note that up until that little speech it had been Mister Jamison. Now it was Jamison.

"Can you make that a little clearer?"

"Biskay came to you. He had a proposition for you. Apparently you accepted it," Barnstock said.

"Just suppose, for the sake of argument, I can't remember a thing about it?"

"You've co-operated beautifully up until now. Without coercion. But coercion is possible."

130

"How?"

Quellan stood up. He was a damn tall man. "Through a
. . . a sister agency, Jamison, the Tampa police department has been advised not to establish any crash priority
to the solution of the fatal shooting of a Mr. Zaragosa,
a foreign national, at Tampa International Airport on
the afternoon of the seventh of· May, twelve days ago.
Nor is the South American government involved eager to
make a big fuss about the death of Alvaro Zaragosa.
The Tampa police have little to work on. We received,
indirectly, what little they have. A rental sedan was
involved in the assassination. Gasoline had been used
to wipe a decal from the door of the sedan. The bottle
which had contained the gasoline was found in the gutter
at the time the sedan was recovered. On the bottle were
two clear fingerprints, the index and middle finger of the
left hand. Tampa's attempt to check them out through
central records resulted in a dead end. When we learned
Biskay had been here with you, we got your prints out
of the military files. Your prints are on the bottle. Tampa
has no way of tracing you. Unless we inform them. Then
they'll want a very complete story, Jamison. It would be
simpler to give it to us."

I looked at my left hand. When I had dropped the
bottle I had expected it to break. But it didn't. I had
tried to stamp it with my heel, but I had missed because it
was rolling, and I had been in a hurry.

I looked at the recorder. "Turn it on," I told Barnstock.
He did.

"What time did he arrive at your house and who answered the door?" Quellan asked.

"It was about six-thirty, I think. I answered the door."

"Now tell us the complete events of the time he was
here, the proposition he made you, and your reaction to
it and your reasons for accepting it."

My mind had raced ahead, and I saw a way out. A
little glimmer of light. I left out the big wad of money. I
left out his detailed analysis of the political climate of the
Peral government and the Melendez insurrection. I told
them that I was broke at the time Biskay made the pro-

131

position, that I was having wife trouble, that I was feeling restless.

"Just what did he want you to do for him?"

"To arrive in my own car in Tampa on Tuesday, May sixth, and check in at the Tampa Terrace Hotel under the name of Robert Martin. Which I did. He had explained to me in April that it wasn't anything particularly illegal. He said the cops wouldn't come into it in any way. I got the impression it was more of a . . . a hijacking operation. All I had to do was be in my car at a certain time and a certain place in Tampa on the afternoon of the sixth. He'd come in another car and then we would get the hell out of there. I was supposed to drive him to Atlanta to the airport there."

"What was his offer?"

"Twenty-five thousand cash."

"Didn't that seem like a great deal of money for just a job of driving?"

"Yes, it did. But he said he had to have somebody he could trust implicitly. And he had elected me. Understand, I didn't jump at it. But he kept telling me nothing could go wrong."

"He came to the hotel on the sixth?"

"Yes. And he went in my car and he showed me where I was to park, near a side entrance to the hospital. He said he would come out that entrance."

"I thought you said he said he would come in another car."

"Did I? That was a mistake. It turned out that he came in another car. He said he'd come out the entrance and I was to watch for him, and start the motor as soon as he arrived. We drove over the route we would take out of town a couple of times."

"Describe what happened."

"I parked where he told me to at quarter after three. The car was gassed up. I kept watching the hospital door. At three forty-five, maybe a couple of minutes later, a black sedan pulled up directly behind me. I didn't know what to think. I looked back and recognized Vince. As I got out of the station wagon, a man got out of the sedan

132

and started walking down the street rapidly. He didn't look back, so I didn't see his face. He was a big man in a gray suit. He wore a chauffeur's hat. The suit could have been a uniform. He carried a small satchel. Vince was bloody. He'd been shot in the leg and the shoulder, but he could walk. He was nearly out on his feet, but anxious to get out of town. He had a big black tin suitcase in the sedan. I put it in the station wagon at his request. Our luggage, Vince's and mine, was already there in the station wagon. We'd put it in at noon. Vince gave me a bottle of fluid and told me to go wipe the decal off the side of the sedan. I did so, and dropped the small bottle in the gutter. I drove out of town fast."

I told them about giving him crude first aid. I told them the places we had stopped, the time we made, about Vince's infection and about bribing the doctor—at Vince's request.

"You must have heard about the murder of Zaragosa. There were enough details in the press and on the radio so that you must have known Biskay was involved in it. Didn't you question him? You didn't contract for anything like that."

"Yes, of course. Vince assured me that he had not killed Zaragosa. He said somebody else had come along with the same idea."

"What idea?"

"Taking whatever it was Zaragosa had."

"The black tin suitcase?"

"I guessed that was it."

"Did he tell you what was in the suitcase?"

"No. I know it was damn heavy."

"When did he give you your money?"

"The first night out of Tampa. In Stark, Florida."

"Did it occur to you the suitcase might contain money?"

"I thought of it, but it seemed too heavy."

"Did he mention any names?"

"Yes. Some woman named Carmela. I read about her in the paper. She was killed when a plane crashed that she was flying. He said it belonged to a man named Melendez, the man he had been working for."

"No other names?"

"Maybe. But I can't remember any."

"How about a man named Kyodos? Did he mention that name?"

"It doesn't ring any bell. I'm not saying he didn't, but I just can't remember."

"What denomination was the money he paid you?"

"Hundreds. All in hundreds. Two hundred and fifty of them. He said the money was safe to spend, that it wasn't marked or anything."

"But you couldn't drive him to Atlanta."

"No. He was too badly hurt to catch the plane he wanted."

"So you offered to let him come to your house again."

I tried to look embarrassed. "It wasn't exactly an offer. I mean I felt that he was asking me to share a risk I didn't know enough about. So I wanted to be paid for taking that risk. So . . . we dickered. And finally agreed on another twenty thousand. In advance."

"What denominations?"

"Just the same. All hundreds."

"And still you hadn't decided the black suitcase held money?"

"I'd become a little more certain it might be money."

"Did you ask him?"

"Yes. Several times. He didn't want to tell me. When he was sick I tried to look in it. It was locked. I thought about busting it open but decided against it. After all, he'd gotten hold of me because he felt he could trust me. And he could trust me. We went through a lot together. I . . . I thought a lot of him until . . . he took off with my wife."

"We'll get to that later, Jamison. Now let's go through the Tampa thing again in more detail. Everything you can remember. I particularly want to know if Biskay seemed very wary, if he had any idea he might be followed."

"He seemed a little jumpy."

"In what way? What did he say to give you that impression? What did he do that led you to believe that?"

And so it went. I stuck to my yarn of the guy in the chauffeur's hat. I couldn't be certain, but I felt that I was getting it across. When I had been able to stick to the truth it had been easy to answer their questions. But with one lie added, I had to keep constantly on the alert to avoid any inconsistency. Yet I had to give the impression of being as relaxed as when I had been telling them of Central Burma. It was singularly exhausting, particularly when they gave the impression of not being entirely satisfied with my story.

At four o'clock there was another ten-minute break. They went into the bedroom and talked in low tones to each other. Then they started again. They were concerned now about what had happened after I had brought Vince back to the house. I had been over it enough times with Paul Heissen so that I felt a little more confident.

Barnstock came up with a jim-dandy question. "Jamison, does it seem inconsistent to you that Biskay should take off with your wife?"

"I don't think I know what you mean."

"You've painted a picture of your wife as a lush, and a tramp. Biskay had made a big haul. He's a clever man. An unreliable woman could be dangerous to him. Isn't she precisely the sort of woman he *wouldn't* take with him?"

They were both looking at me intently. I swallowed. "I see what you mean. Of course. But he wasn't in good physical shape. And she had transportation. I suppose he could figure that . . . they could go hole up somewhere until he was able to take off alone. He knew from the clipping I showed him that he had to take off. And I certainly was in no mood to help him. You can understand that. Hell, maybe he even made her an offer of money. She's pretty . . . greedy."

They seemed to buy it, but I couldn't be certain. They moved to other questions. At seven we went to my house. I got the money from the bureau. Quellan read the serial numbers onto the tape. I thought they were going to im-

pound it. Instead it was handed back to me. I stood, holding it, staring stupidly at them.

"I guess you earned it, Jamison," Barnstock said in a
nasty way. "You better declare it as income. That wraps
it up for now. Maybe we'll be back."

I walked to the front hallway with them.

"Is it against the rules for you guys to enlighten me a
little about what's going on?"

They turned on me with identical expressions of cold
amusement. Quellan looked questioningly at Barnstock,
who nodded.

Quellan said, "Your old pal used you for a sucker,
Jamison. We're in it because of the international implications. We've got to prove that the Federal Government
had no part of any secret deal to sell or supply arms to
anybody. Biskay used you to help lift some very heavy
funds. At least a million. Maybe five. He had his hidey
hole all planned. And, my friend, several groups of very
rough people know there was that much and very probably know who lifted it. And they will go to great lengths
to get hold of that much money. We traced you. They
can trace you. I think you're standing out in the cold
cold breeze, boy. They won't use a tape recorder. They'll
want a lead on Biskay and the black suitcase. They'll keep
asking."

I watched them walk out to the curb and get into the
job with the tail fins and turn on the lights and roll away.
The street was empty. The shadows under the trees were
black. I locked the front door and the back door and I
cursed Vince Biskay. And myself.

I called Paul Heissen. They said he was home. I called
his home. I asked him if it would be okay if I went away
for a little while. He was polite and very firm. He said no.
He said if I took off, I would be brought back. I slammed
the phone down onto the cradle.

Chapter 12

Barnstock and Quellan had interrogated me on Monday, the nineteenth of May. There was nothing I could do but wait. The days went by. I could not tell whether they had just been attempting to frighten me, or whether I was actually in danger. Yet every time I thought of Vince it seemed more possible that he had set me up for his friends to knock over. I did not go out at night. I played golf at the club, but my timing was off and my concentration was spotty. In the evenings I tried to read but I would find myself losing the sense of what I read. I refused the invitations of those friends who felt that they had to cheer me up.

Paul Heissen came and talked to me several times. There was, of course, no word about Lorraine. On a Wednesday, the twenty-eighth, Paul had me come downtown and make a formal statement. He mentioned that he had gotten the key to Camp Sootsus from E. J. and had gone up and looked around. Lorraine apparently hadn't been there.

The human organism cannot sustain tension very long. I began to feel listless and depressed. Once I phoned Liz Addams at her home. As soon as she understood who it was, she hung up on me. And I began to drink more heavily. Not to complete drunkenness. But to the point where the edges and outlines of things were softened and bearable, from morning until night.

At times I thought of the money, of the fat brown packages in the bottom of the packing case, sleeping there, nestled and content, dreaming of yachts and rings, women and kings, wines and spices and far-off places. And, for a time, by concentrating on the money, I was able to summon up the goose-pimply hollowness in the belly, the quick and shallow breathing of excitement. But it was a jaded descendant of the emotion I had felt when I had first seen the money. And after a time I was unable to achieve any quickening when I thought of it. It was money, wrapped and hidden. I was rich beyond any previous promptings of avarice. One day I sat at the living-room desk and computed what return I could get from the money were it invested. Two hundred and sixteen thousand a year. About seven hundred a day. But it slept there in the crate in storage, its big muscles slack. It gave me the frantic feeling of wasting time. But I could not leave. I was forced to wait. I could try to leave, but it would be stupid to be on the run, to be a hunted man. I told myself that one day soon Paul would clear me officially. In the meantime I was existing. Whenever my wallet was nearly empty, I would take another two bills from the bureau hoard. I tried not to change too many of them at the same place. My expenses were not large. The money would last me a long time. Long enough.

As window dressing, I made a date with Archie Brill and went to his office and talked about divorce. He said I could start proceedings in about two years.

After I left his office I stopped in a bar and looked at myself in the back bar mirror. Archie had told me I wasn't looking very well. The mirror was blue. I looked beat. Gaunt face and hollow eyes, and the lines very deep around my mouth. I would lie awake nights in the dark guest room and listen to my heart, to the sharp and rapid beat that came out of bottles. There was an emptiness in my life I could not fill. The world spun slowly into the endless heat of summer, and every day was like the one behind it and the one in front of it. I had told Irene I didn't need her any longer. The house was dusty and dirty, and the grass grew long and rank in the yard. Tinker phoned me a few times, obviously wanting to be asked over. I did not want to see her.

I remember one evening in particular. I was drunk. And at midnight I found myself with the phone at my ear, listening to the dial tone, filled with a fierce compulsion to call someone, anyone, and say, "I killed them. Both of them."

I pulled myself together with a long shuddering effort, completely shaken by the narrowness of my escape. For the first time in my life I understood the curious compulsion to confess.

I went to my bedroom and did something I had not done since I was a child. I knelt beside my bed. I clasped my hands, bent my head, closed my eyes and tried to pray.

"God help me," I said.

There was no answer. I was an emptiness kneeling and praying to emptiness. The floor hurt my knees.

"Who am I?" I asked.

And heard my own answer. Murderer. Thief. Libertine. Drunkard.

I laid my empty body and empty soul in the bed and yearned for the momentary oblivion of sleep.

The next day I was vastly restless. I walked a dozen miles through the empty cluttered rooms. In the last hour of daylight a short and violent thunderstorm came down on the city. I watched it from the living-room windows. The house was like a sturdy boat moving on even keel through gale winds. It cleared and the storm grumbled off into the southwest, and for a short time the last of the sun turned the world to gold. I had a curious feeling of expectancy, as though I was on the verge of some great revelation. I dressed most carefully and went out and got into the car and drove away, with no destination in mind.

Chapter 13

The place was called the Sidewheeler. I had been there twice, possibly three times before. It was about eighteen miles south of Vernon, and just over the state line, and in a wide-open county. The other times I had been there it had been with a group, after a cocktail party. There was a six-lane divided highway and, for about a mile and a half on either side of it, neon yelped in bright delirium.

There were cabins and bars and clubs and motels and drive-ins and package stores and eateries and strippers and motels and gift shops and pinball galleries and floor shows and casinos.

The area was a vast asphalt scab on the valley floor, and it was known as the Greenwood Strip. The Side-wheeler had the most pretentious layout, a uniformed man to park your car in a huge lot, a blue neon line drawing of a riverboat with a turning paddle wheel. The décor carried out the motif of the sign and the name, with portholes, brass bells and ships' wheels, navigation charts and red and green running lights, and, in the game room, croupiers dressed like Mississippi gamblers. It was well known in Vernon that there wasn't an honest game along the strip, that the cheaper bars were infested with B girls. But, as with most areas where the gambling is heavy, the Sidewheeler and the other three or four top places served generous drinks and excellent food at a reasonable price. And enticed some almost big names into the floor shows.

I surrendered the wagon to the man in uniform and pocketed my claim check and went into the calculatedly obscure lighting of the bar. Trade was good. As I had had nothing but coffee all day, the second generous martini made my lips feel numb. I sat on my bar stool and looked at the pale shoulders of the women, the intent faces of their men. I seemed to sit in a private little area of personal silence where I could listen to all of the sounds at once, the busy aviary of the words and laughter of women, the clink and tinkle of ice on glass, of silver on china. Whirr of the electric daiquiri maker. Muted rumble of truck on the highway. Clack of ice in the professional shaker. Blur of male voices.

In the blue gloom the place was full of tiny highlights. On rings and earrings and bracelets and lighters and drinks and cuff links. The highlights moved and changed.

And faces bent toward the abrupt orange flames of matches and lighters.

The party at my left moved on into the dining room when the headwaiter told them their table was ready. The bar stools were taken quickly. I ordered the third drink.

The voice on my left said, "Ever see this one?"

I turned and looked at him. He was young and big, in a gray seersucker jacket, a blue sports shirt open at the throat. He had a cropped blond Prussian head, a fleshy face, small eyes. He looked like a recent All-American mention after three years on the road and ten thousand drinks. I suspected that if the light was better, I could see the small broken veins in his nose and cheeks.

"See what?" I asked. He had his big hand closed.

"Got a fly in here. A high class fly. The only kind you can catch in a joint like this. Now watch."

He had the water chaser that had come with his straight shot. It was half full. He clapped his palm over the top of the glass. The live housefly flew down into the water. It buzzed on the top. The man took a swizzle stick and poked it under. Soon it gave up all movement.

"You follow me?" he said.

"So what? You caught a fly and you drowned it. Bully for you."

"Now what if he stays in there ten minutes, under water? I ask you this. Is he dead?"

"You're damn well told he's dead."

He looked at his watch. "It's ten after eight. I take him out at twenty after. You say he'll be dead."

"He's dead already."

He took out his wallet, selected a twenty-dollar bill and put it on the bar top. "I say he'll be alive."

"That fly will be alive?"

"And he'll fly away."

"No play on words, friend. No substituting flies."

"How the hell could I do that? No. No gag. That fly will fly away, pal."

I put my twenty on top of his. When about eight minutes had gone by he asked the nearest bartender for a salt shaker. When the ten minutes were up, he fished the

141

fly out with the swizzle stick, tapped it off on the bar top. He lit a match so we could see it better, a shapeless black blob.

"Dead?"

"It sure is."

"Don't reach for the money," he said. He covered the fly with a mound of salt until it was completely concealed. "Now keep an eye on him."

I watched the mound of salt. Nothing happened. The man ordered a new shot and a fresh chaser. I sipped my martini. Suddenly the surface of the mound of salt stirred. Then the salt blew away with a tiny explosion as the fly burst out and flew away. The man picked up the money and tucked it in his wallet. "Learned that in San Antone two years ago," he said. "Bet I've made over fifteen hundred bucks. Buy you a drink."

"Okay. It was fair and square. I'll be damned."

"Salt dries them out fast. Fifteen minutes is too long. Roy Macksie is my name."

"Jerry Jamison." We shook hands.

He tore off six paper matches and put them on the bar. "Five bucks says you can't arrange those matches so they form four equilateral triangles."

"No thanks."

"That's a money maker too, Jerry." We talked. He said he sold heavy construction equipment. The second sip of the fifth drink made me gag. I said I had to eat or fall on my face.

"I'm hungry too," he said, "but let's not eat here. There's a place down the strip that has a hell of a good steak. Okay?"

"Okay by me, Roy."

We picked up our change, left tips on the bar and went out into the busy night. I was ahead of him. There was a canopied entrance and two shallow steps. There was a hard and meaningful nudge in the small of my back.

"Now, Jerry, down the steps and straight out to the curb."

142

The uniformed man was ten feet away. "Car check, gentlemen?" he said.

"We'll be back later," Macksie said.

"What the hell?" I said.

"Right out to the curb. Want you to meet some friends. Want to talk about Vince."

I walked. I knew my reflexes were dull. I could remember a lot of things I had been taught long ago, but I guessed he had learned in the same school because the metal hardness did not touch my back again. I reached the curb. Traffic was heavy. When there was a gap in traffic, I did not move forward at his command. I waited for him to nudge me again. The moment he did so, I leaned back against the gun muzzle so as to maintain contact with it, and at the same time, spun to my left, swinging my right arm in a hard arc, fingers open, estimating the level of his throat. It worked with a perfection I had not expected. I chopped him just under the jaw with the edge of my hand. He did not sway or stagger. He went down like a big puppet when the strings are cut, feet in grass, belly across the curbing, face smacking asphalt with a meaty sound, right hand still in the pocket of the seersucker jacket. Oncoming traffic whirred by and I saw the pale ovals of faces turned to look at the roadside tableau. I stood there a moment, uncertain as to what to do next. And saw two men coming swiftly across the far lanes toward me through the eerie yellow glow of sodium vapor lights. They were halted by traffic on my side. I turned and ran. I ran along the edge of the highway toward the oncoming lights, my feet making a leathery slapping noise on the paving. I had the feeling that I floated along without effort, swift as the wind.

Until I stumbled and nearly fell and heard the ragged gasping of my breath and began to feel the clinch of pain in my left side. I looked back and saw no one and walked swiftly toward a jumble of confusing lights ahead.

Most of the businesses fronted on the highway. There was a gap between a bar and a darkened store. It had been turned into an entrance to a carnival set up in the wide field behind the businesses along the strip. I walked into the heavy pedestrian traffic that moved slowly up and down the small midway. Strings of lights and the bright glare of gasoline lanterns. Dull roar of generators competing with brass music and the amplified brag and wheedle of the talkers, and the glissanding roar of the rides. Sawdust and sweat and cotton candy and three balls for a dime, you can't lose, and the lazy humid young hips under the cotton skirts, and babies asleep with their heads bobbling on the shoulders of young husbands, and roving gangs of teens, and the snapping of the crooked captive rifles killing the plywood ducks. I moved at their pace through stinks of beer, perfume, sweat, by the blurry lights, past the romp and halloo, on undone legs, my left side full of knives.

I edged out of the throng to a quiet corner where I could stand with my back toward the illusion of safety of taut worn canvas, and looked back the way I had come, looked back toward the garish temporary arch, waiting for them. I remembered how they had looked coming across the highway, swift and black under the poisonous yellow of the lights—as unreal as Dick Tracy. And in the same directness, their look of purpose was the same thing I had seen in front of the air terminal as they had come toward Vince and Zaragosa. I wondered if they were the same. Sweat began to dry. Breathing became slower. My legs did not tremble as much. I lit a cigarette. And watched.

The girl appeared suddenly beside me. I had not seen her approach me. Red bullfighter pants. Soiled ankles. Hair bleached hard and white. Mouth painted square. Big breasts swelling a white satin blouse. Broad patient face and practiced bovine eyes. Seventeen or thirty, or anything in between. Red purse with sequins, many missing.

"Maybe we both got stood up, hey?" she said, her voice deep and rough.

"Maybe," I said. They would look for a man alone.

"My name is Bobbie."

"Hi, Bobbie. I'm Joe."

144

"Hi, Joe."

We weighed and studied each other for that timeless moment, that ancient recognition. What passes for pride had been eased by the trite gambit of the approach.

"I got a trailer," she said.

"That's nice. That's handy."

She had looked at my clothes, my shoes. "Twennyfi' bucks."

"All right."

"I like a guy don't try to argue and chisel the price."

I wanted to tell her there was something refreshing about such directness, after Tinker and Mandy. I went with her. She had found my hand and we walked holding hands. When we came to a narrow place, she went ahead, her fleshy hips rolling in an exaggerated way in the tight red fabric. We went out of the lights to a back area, between ropes and stakes and guy lines. A group of men sat around a packing case playing cards in the hard white light of a gasoline lantern.

When we passed close one of them said, "Good evenin', Bobbie," his voice slow and deep and dignified.

"Hi, Andy," she said. They continued their game. No jeers or whistles. To each his own function and occupation.

The trailers were clumped fifty yards away. There were lights in some of them. I heard the jackal voice of a comedian, and then the prolonged roar of studio applause and laughter. Her trailer was aluminum, and small and road-weary. It was off the hitch. A gray sedan was parked next to it. She knocked on the door, listened to the silence, and then unlocked it, turned on a light—a big bulb in a vivid orange shade. Like being inside a musky pumpkin. She latched the door behind us, adjusted venetian blinds to close out all of the night.

"Make yourself comfortable, Joe. We got some bourbon. You want a drink?"

"No thanks. I've had all I can handle."

"Well, you don't act it. Mind if I fix myself one?"

"Go right ahead." I sat in the only chair. It was small and uncomfortable. She knelt in front of the tiny kitchen unit, put two cubes of ice in a green plastic glass, dumped bourbon in liberally, carried her drink to the bunk and sat on it, facing me.

"Here's lookin' up your address," she said. She drank and sighed and said, "I needed this one."

"Do you drive and haul this trailer around?"

"They won't let me drive. I'm a lousy driver they keep telling me. That's Charlie and Carol Ann. Charlie is Carol Ann's boy friend. Charlie owns the Whip and the Caterpillar. I tell you they're the only honest to God friends I ever had. They've been swell to me. There's nobody taking a slice off the top so I get to pick and choose. I wouldn't wanna bring no bums in here, you understand. No rough stuff. I liked the way you looked, you know."

"Sure. Thanks."

"That's okay. You're welcome." She set the empty glass aside, yawned and began to unbutton her blouse. "You want we should have the light on?"

"Hold it, Bobbie. That isn't what I have in mind."

She tensed and her eyes turned hard and suspicious. "What the hell do you have in mind? I don't go for any specialties, buster."

I took out my wallet. I found a five and a twenty and handed her the two bills. She took them and said, "Now what?" She was still suspicious.

I took out the claim check on my car. "I want you to do me a favor. I'll give you another twenty bucks."

"What's on your mind?"

"You know the Sidewheeler?"

"Sure. Just down the road. I never been in it."

"I've been trying to get away from some people who've been bothering me. I don't want to run into them. I want you to take this claim check to the doorman and ask for my car. I'll give you a full description of it and the license number. He'll probably ask. Tell him the owner is sick and sent you after his car. He'll let you have it. Give him this dollar. Then bring the car back here."

"It is a hot car?"

146

"No."

"Let me see the registration." I took it out of the wallet and handed it to her. "You're Jerome Jamison?" she asked.

"Yes."

"What kind of trouble can I get into on this deal?"

"No trouble. I just want to get away from those people."

"They'll recognize your car, won't they?"

"Keep an eye out and see if you're followed. If you are, don't come back here with it. Put it in the lot across from the carnival and come back through the midway and bring me the car keys."

She thought it over and shook her head. "I won't do it. Not for twenty bucks."

"What will you do it for?"

"I'll do it for fifty bucks."

"What makes you think it's worth fifty bucks?"

"I'm just guessing."

I took out two more twenties and a ten. Handed them to her. She put the money away and said, "So okay, friend. Only I better be dressed a little different to go up to the front of that joint, don't you think?"

"It might make it easier."

"I got a suit I can put on." She opened the very narrow door of a tiny closet, took out a dark blue suit on a hanger and laid it on the bed. The trailer was so small that I could have reached out and touched her as she stood with her back to me and unzipped the red bullfighter pants and peeled them down. She turned and sat on the bed to pull them off her legs. As she stepped into the skirt, pulled it up and zipped it, she said, "You sure this hasn't got anything to do with the cops?"

"I'm certain."

She tucked the satin blouse into the waistband of the skirt, put the jacket on and gave her hair a couple of quick pats. "Okay?"

"Fine."

I walked out into the night with her. "Which direction will you come from, Bobbie?"

"Over there. You have to go all the way around in back and come in over the railroad tracks."

"I'll be waiting," I said.

I saw her go. The night swallowed her. Then she reappeared again in the carnival lights, walking quickly in her blue suit. Five minutes to walk to the Sidewheeler. Three minutes to get the car. Five minutes to drive back. Certainly no more than fifteen minutes if it went smoothly.

I opened the trailer door and turned the orange light out. I closed it and leaned against the side of the trailer. I lit a cigarette. The blare and rumble of the carnival was softened by distance. The sky was clear, the stars bright. Two women with hacksaw voices quarreled in a nearby trailer. You said you did. I never said I did. You wasn't listening or something. I damn well heard you say you did. Oh, shut up, for once. I won't shut up. I heard you tell Pete you did it. I never told Pete nothing.

After about ten minutes had gone by, I moved away from the trailer, snapped the butt away, moved into the deeper shadow by a battered stake truck.

The headlights appeared suddenly as the car came across the railroad tracks. It moved slowly across the open field toward the trailer. I saw that it was my wagon. But I wanted to be certain no other car followed it. It stopped forty feet away from me, next to Bobbie's trailer. She left the lights on and the motor running and got out.

Just as I started to move toward her, she turned and said, "I told you he said he'd wait right here."

"Ssshh!"

I turned to move away as quickly and silently as I could. I tripped and fell headlong across a flat bed trailer into a mass of jangling metal. I scrambled to my feet. I heard the running footsteps close behind me. I tried to dodge away but someone ran into me and we both went down on the rank grass. I struck out at him and hit him once and then there was a great blow against my head, just behind my ear. It flashed behind my eyes like nearby lightning. I did not go out completely. I was aware of being pulled to my feet. I knew there was one

148

on each side of me, that both my wrists were painfully locked against the small of my back. I could walk in a spongy way.

Then we were beside my car. The headlights against the aluminum trailer made a reflected glow. Bobbie said, "What're you doin' to him? What're you gonna do to him? You didn't say you were goin' to . . ."

And a blurred shadow moved quickly and savagely, and I heard the wet crunch of the blow against her face, saw her run backward into the side of the trailer and fall. And heard her begin to whine, a helpless animal sound. I tried to plunge away from them, but they held me effortlessly. The first blow had weakened me.

"Turn him a little. Okay. Hold it."

The side wall of my head tottered and fell in upon itself with a prolonged rumbling crash that turned out every light in the world.

Chapter 14

I woke up in the middle of the night with a horrible headache. I looked at a familiar light pattern on the ceiling and realized that Lorraine had gotten up to go to the bathroom and had left the bathroom door ajar. Wherever the party had been, it had been a dandy.

Best thing to do is roll over and try to go back to sleep. I tried to roll over and I could not. It startled me. As I began to investigate I found that I was fully dressed, that I lay spread-eagled on my bed, wrists and ankles tied somehow to the four corners of the bed.

So the party had been at our house and I had passed out and some comical type had tied me up.

"Lorraine?" Then, a bit louder, "Lorraine!"

No answer. No guarantee that she was even in the house. If the party had moved on somewhere, she would be with it. Maybe she had dreamed up the idea of tying me up. It would certainly give her more freedom of action.

Try to sleep anyway.

I tried. I could not. I was too uncomfortable. I heard a noise downstairs. Somebody down there.

"Hey!" I yelled. "Hey, anybody!"

And footsteps came up the stairs fast. More than one set. Somebody came in and fumbled around for the light switch and finally found it. I blinked at the sudden brightness and smiled sheepishly and said, "Somebody with a cute sense of humor fixed me up good. Untie me, will you, please?"

Three men had come into the bedroom. I didn't recognize any of them. One was big and beefy and blond. Maybe one of Lorraine's new friends. The other two weren't her type. Small and dark and wiry, and too sharply dressed. Nobody smiled.

"Get me loose, will you? Where's Lorraine?"

The big blond one stood at the foot of the bed and looked down at me. The side of his face looked as though he had recently taken a bad fall.

"That was real cute, Jamison, sending that little tailpiece back after your car. But for another thirty bucks she cooperated very very nicely."

I stared at him blankly. "I don't know what you're talking about. Who the hell are you? Where is my wife?"

"Nice act," the big one said. "We want the money. Where is it?"

And then I got the picture. This was robbery. They had a lot of nerve to come in and tie me up like this. I wondered what they'd done to Lorraine.

"Listen," I said. "We don't keep money around the house. A few bucks, but not important money. You're welcome to what we've got."

One of the small dark ones spoke to the other in a language I couldn't identify. The one spoken to reached into his inside pocket and pulled out the thickest wad of hundred dollar bills I'd ever seen outside a bank. He framed them and said, "We found this much, Jamison. Where's the rest of it?"

"The rest of what? You never found that much in this house."

They all looked down at me for a little while, and then they moved away from the bed and talked in low tones. I was worried about Lorraine. If she was still out, she might walk in on this. They might hurt her. She wouldn't know how to handle a situation like this. The smart thing was to let them have what they wanted.

They made a decision. They got a blue plastic sponge out of the bathroom. The bedroom blinds were closed. The big one pressed hard with his thumbs against the hinges of my jaw, forcing my mouth open. One of the others forced the sponge into my mouth. They tied it in place with one of my neckties. They took off my right shoe and sock, and tied my ankle more firmly. One of the dark ones opened a pocket knife, sat on the bed with his back to me, and began to work on my naked foot.

Until the pain began I could not help thinking it was some kind of an involved joke. I was wondering if one of my friends had hired these boys to scare me half to death. But when the pain started, it all became real. I tried to keep it away from me. I tried to push down, so the pain would stay there in my foot. But it came up and it became a part of me and there was nothing but pain. I roared against the sponge. I bucked and screamed, eyes bulging, but he didn't stop. And I swung hard around a dizzy curve and slammed down into darkness. And came to with the tears drying on my face, and they looked at me and he started again, his narrow back hunched over my bare foot. The other two did not watch him. I tore at the bonds until my shoulders creaked and my hands went numb. I made soundless shrieks and passed out again. When I came to the sponge was gone. My foot felt as though I were holding it in a bed of coals, but the pain was dull enough to bear.

"The rest of the money," the big one said.

I had little wind, as though I had run a long way. "I don't know what you're talking about. This . . . is some kind of a mistake. You can have anything you want. Don't . . . hurt me again like that."

"You get hurt again and again and again," the big one said. "We've got all the time there is. Again and again and again, until we get the money."

One of the small dark ones, the one who hadn't worked on my foot, said, "Hold it a minute." He turned on the bed lamp, put his hand on my chin and turned my face toward the light and looked into my eyes.

"What is the date, Jamison?" He had an accent I couldn't place.

"Let me think. April. Sometime in April."

"What did you do yesterday?"

"Yesterday? I worked, I guess." I tried to remember yesterday. I could not remember anything about it with any distinctness.

"When did you last see Vincente Biskay?"

"Vince? My God, it's been . . . thirteen years. But . . ."

"But what?"

"I just had the funny feeling that I'd seen him recently. Just for a moment. With a ring on his finger with a red stone in it. But that's nonsense."

"Are you falling for that?" the big one asked.

"You are too heavy-handed, my friend," the one who had questioned me said. "I don't think our friend is bright enough to simulate a classic case of traumatic amnesia. I suspect you gave him a nice little concussion. And I do not think he would stand so much pain so well."

The big one looked dismayed. "What does it mean?"

"It means there will be a return of memory, either bit by bit or all at once. In ten minutes, ten days, or ten weeks. Until then there isn't a thing we can do."

"Memory of what?" I asked.

The little one looked down at me with no expression. He glanced at his wrist. "It is three in the morning on Saturday the fourteenth day of June," he said.

I stared at him without comprehension. "Are you crazy?"

"I'm not lying to you. You have a lot to remember. Start with Biskay. Try to remember Biskay. And try to remember money. A great deal of money."

"Who are you? What do you want?"

152

"We'll wait until you remember."

"Where's my wife?"

"She's no longer here. She hasn't been here for over a month."

"Where is she? Where the hell is she?"

"Nobody seems to know."

They had another whispered conference in a far corner of the room. The one who had damaged my foot dressed it deftly, using gauze from the medicine cabinet. He and the big one left. I heard them go down the stairs. The other one stared at me for a little while, lips pursed, and then followed them, turning the light out as he left the room.

Biskay and money. I wondered how Vince was, wondered what he had been doing all these years. The fourteenth of June. Two months gone. I could not believe it. I tried to make myself believe it, tried to capture lost memories. When I was small we had a small gray cat for nearly a year. Its name was Misty. For weeks after it was run over, I kept seeing it out of the corner of my eye, just out of my range of vision. And I would turn, but of course it was not there because I had watched my father bury it, and I had put up a cross for it.

These memories were like that gray cat. They seemed to be there, but as soon as I could catch the hint of one and try to face it directly, it would be gone.

One memory, or pseudo-memory, was clear long enough for me to grasp it. There was sunlight in the bedroom. Tinker Velbiss sat naked at the dressing table, brushing her red hair. That, of course, was absurd.

And then something about a copper screen, holes in a screen. But that was gone too.

I wondered if the man had lied to me about Lorraine. Why would she go away? Where could she go?

My foot throbbed and burned. And I felt the growth of a cold anger, an anger born of pain and humiliation and indignity. No matter what had happened in the lost months, these men had no right to do this to me. And it seemed easier and more satisfying to think of how to untie myself than to try to explore memories that were not there. I tested my good foot and my hands carefully, each in turn. I could touch the bonds with my fingers. It felt as though they had used neckties. It was a Hollywood bed with a stubby headboard, no footboard. From the angle of my wrists, it seemed that the other ends of the bonds were tied to the frame. They had left the bed lamp on the bedside table lighted, but I could not lift my head high enough to see either wrist.

I pulled myself as far to my right as I could. I pulled until I felt that I was dislocating my left shoulder. It gave me a few inches of slack on the right wrist. I moved my right arm back and forth as far as the slack permitted, rubbing the binding against the metal edge of the bed frame. It slid smoothly. I strained to change the angle. After several attempts I felt a small catch of fabric on an edge or roughness of metal. I worked at it, resting from time to time. I felt the tiny rippings, the threads being pulled loose. Yet when I yanked hard at it, it held firm. The frequent yanking had forced the wrist loop so tight my hand was numb. The awkward position made an agony in the stretched muscles of my arm and shoulder.

I felt that I could not free myself. I gave a final convulsive effort, using the last of my fading strength. There was a sudden rip and pop of taut fabric and my arm was free. I laid it across my belly and rested for a time, breathing hard, feeling the strain and pain go out of the muscles. I loosened the wrist knot with my teeth and then lay quietly, working my numb fingers, feeling the needles of sensation return.

I rolled onto my left shoulder, reached over and, in a few minutes, released my left wrist. I sat up, massaging my hands, rubbing my arms. And heard footsteps on the stairs.

There was a heavy glass ashtray on the bedside table. I picked it up with my left hand and lay back, spreading my arms as before, the ashtray out of sight over the far edge of the bed. I could only hope that it was one of them, and he would not turn on the main lights. I turned my head toward the door and closed my eyes, not completely, left them open just enough to see him vaguely. And as he came in, I groaned.

He came to the bed. He leaned over me, just enough to be within the sweeping circle of my right arm. I swung it around and caught the nape of his neck and smashed the heavy ashtray full into his face. It fell from my hand onto my belly. He made a pale sound, moving weakly. I picked it up again and swung it against his face. This time it shattered. He was one of the dark ones, not the one who had worked on my foot. He collapsed across me, slipping back toward the floor. I held him and lowered him gently to the floor beside the bed. His face was finished for all time. I strained over the side of the bed and went through his clothing. There was no gun on him. There was a pocket knife, a tiny gold thing, flat, with a single blade. I used it to cut my ankles free. I hitched myself to the end of the bed and sat there for a moment steeling myself to the point where I could chance putting my weight on the damaged foot. I stood with all my weight on my left leg and tentatively pressed my right foot against the floor. The room swam and tilted and I sat down again. I tried again. I was able to bear it, though it made me sick and dizzy.

The toy knife was not a weapon. I remembered my .22 automatic, wondered why it had not occurred to me sooner. I hobbled to the bureau. It was gone from its usual place in the drawer. I had thrown it into . . . And the memory was gone. Something about darkness. I shook my head in a vain effort to clear it, but only awakened an area of pain behind my left ear. I touched it with my fingertips. It had the pressure and sensitivity of an infection, and the feeling of heat.

I took a sock from my bureau drawer and went into the bathroom, taking small quick steps on the damaged foot. When I turned the bathroom light on I saw Lorraine before me on the floor, her head at a sick angle. I gasped with shock and then she faded abruptly and was gone. It was as though I had stared fixedly at her for a long time and then turned quickly and saw the retinal after-image of her on the bare tile floor in that

155

moment before it faded and was gone. I felt as if I were losing my mind.

I opened the medicine cabinet and took a jar of cream deodorant and slipped it down into the toe of the sock. It was of heavy glass. When I swung the sock it had a lethal weight.

There were two more of them. Two that I knew about. The big one and the one who had worked on my foot. But there could be more. I went into the bedroom and looked at the one on the floor. He seemed to be breathing very slowly and very heavily. I turned out the table lamp and went to the bedroom phone. I heard the dial tone. I dialed zero. The operator answered. I asked for police headquarters.

"Police headquarters, Sergeant Ascher."

"Let me talk to Lieutenant Heissen." I heard my own hushed voice ask for a name I had never heard before. Someone I did not know. There had been a Heissen a long time ago. Paul. A brave and stubborn and immovable high school center.

"He isn't on duty."

Fear came from some inexplicable source. Something in the guts. Frail and crackling, like paper too close to a fire, writhing and browning in the heat.

The sergeant was saying, "Hello? Hello?" as I gently replaced the phone on the cradle. I could not understand or rationalize the fear. I was in a train as it plunged through a long tunnel. I saw the tunnel lights whip by me, illuminating fragments of scenes I could not understand.

And I heard another one on the stairs.

I moved as quickly as I could and brought too much weight on my right foot so that for a few moments I was in a great hollow place full of echoes and little dots of brilliance whirled and swam behind my eyes. I did not fall. I moved to the far side of the door, and when the tall shadow came in through the doorway, I swung the heavy sock with all the furious strength of panic. And felt and heard the hard glass jar fragment against the skull. And sensed, beyond that, the sick crumbling

156

of the skull itself. I moved to catch him, but my weight came wrong on my right foot and he was too heavy and he slipped away and fell with a heaviness that filled the night and the silence.

There was a hoarse call from downstairs, a call of panic and question and alarm. I was on my knees in darkness. Clumsy hands on his clothing, fumbling, pawing. He was on his face. Levered him over with grunt of effort. Bulk of metal under the breast of the coat. Cold serrated grip that fitted into the chill oiled sweat of the palm of my hand. The gun felt long and muzzle-heavy. I moved on my knees toward the doorway, struck the dead foot, fell forward, half in and half out of the bedroom. The lower hall light was on. When he reached the head of the stairs, an instant after I fell, he was in silhouette. The trigger pull was stiff. It fired. A most curious sound. A smothered sound. The way a man in church might muffle a cough in his Sunday handkerchief.

The man at the head of the stairs was taking a step forward. He touched his toe to the floor and then swung his foot back, so that it was like a dance step, quite slow. He took another step back and his back was against the wall and he made a long frightened sound. "Maaaaaamm!" he cried, lost and goatlike.

And I fired twice again. Each time the sound was appreciably louder, but the last was no louder than the sound a book would make dropped flat on a rug. Then he took half an aimless step toward the stairs, bowed with an antique grace, plunged. I listened to the inconsequential rattle and thumble of his fall, heard him come to rest in silence. Heard a tiny gagging noise and then nothing.

Tunes came into my mind and I felt my lips spread back in the kind of grin that you acquire when you bump into somebody with an awkward carelessness. Long long ago there was a picture of a murderer. With a song of his own. "Mighty Like a Rose." I whistled it between my teeth, a tinny sound in the silent house. Just the refrain. Over and over. I backed on my hands and knees into the room and touched the muzzle of the gun to the head of the big one, backed off an inch and pulled the trigger. Don't know what to call him but he's mighty like a rose. And the same to the one with the ruined face. The big one did not move when I fired. The dark one bucked and drummed his heels and flapped at the floor with one hand and sighed. I wondered what dreams the leaden pellet had smashed, down into what dark corridors it had dived. Don't know what to call him, but . . .

I turned on a light. I did not look at them. I put a sock on my torn foot with utmost tenderness, and edged it gingerly into my shoe, biting my lip against the pain. I laced it snugly. It was easier to stand on, but when I came to the stairs I inched down them, one at a time, good foot first. The third one lay in the front hall under the light, face down, arm buckled under him, ankles comfortably crossed. Eenie, meenie, minie, mose—you're all mighty like a rose. And drove a round hole into the back of his neck, directly in the center, neat as a strike into the pocket, a long putt, a threaded needle. Then looked up the stairs and saw, before she faded away, a woman naked, struggling with a robe.

By the electric clock in the kitchen it was quarter after four. The keys were not in my car. I had to go through their pockets. I had luck. They were in the pocket of the one in the downstairs hall.

I got into the car.

And suddenly a lot of it came back. It came in heavy clods and jagged pieces. I was like a man who stands under a collapsing building, shielding his head with his arms, waiting for the great roof section that will smash him against the ground. I waited under it until the sound of falling ended. And I looked at what had fallen. There was more to come down. But I had parts of it now. The copper Porsche turning in the air as it fell into the lake. Carrying Lorraine out to the station wagon. Tinker and Mandy. Paul Heissen.

And the money. The thick rich stacks of currency baled with wire, neatly fitted into the black tin suitcase.

I had to have the money, and I had to leave. Quickly.

And I thought of the money and remembered where it was.

I drove out to Park Terrace. I parked by a high stack of cinder block. I used a broken piece of block to break the lock on a tool shed. I knew the right place. A pick and a shovel would be enough. There were stars to see by. The concrete was pale. I tried to swing the pick with great force, but there was no strength in me. I could do little more than lift it with great effort and let it fall under its own weight. When it landed tilted a little one way or the other, the haft would turn in my hands and it would clang on the concrete. After a long time I got to my knees and felt of the hole. It was half the size of an apple, with the concrete around it pocked by the times I had missed my aim.

There was nothing in all the world but the money in the ground and the need to get to it. My clothes were soaked with sweat. Sometimes I fell. When I fell I would lie there and wait until I could get up again and pick up the pick. Finally the point went through into the dirt underneath. I paused and looked around. The world was gray. I had not seen the night go, or the stars. The haft of the pick was sleek and sticky with blood. I walked to the shack and got a long pry bar. On the way back with it I fell and in a little while I got up again. With the pry bar I could break off pieces of the concrete. With the pry bar I was able to break the strand of the reinforcing mesh.

When the hole was as big as the top of a bushel basket, a voice said, "What the hell are you doing, Jerry?"

I turned and stared at him. It was Red Olin. And the sun was well up. I hadn't seen it come up.

"I have to get the money, Red."

"What money? What are you talking about."

"I buried it here before you poured the slab. It's in a black tin suitcase. It's a hell of a lot of money."

"You look sick."

"It's a lot of money, Red. Three million something. I forget just how much. In cash. I've got to get it and get away from here."

He smiled at me. "Sure. You've got to get away from here. That's right."

I smiled back at him. I've always gotten along fine with Red. We've worked well together. We understand each other. "Once you start killing people, Red, you've got to get away."

"That's right."

"How about helping me? I'll give you some of it."

"Sure. I'll help you, Jerry. Glad to."

"It'll go faster with two."

"I'll be back in a couple of minutes, Jerry. You keep right on digging for that money."

"Where are you going?"

"Well . . . I didn't get my coffee yet. I can dig better after my coffee. I could bring you some."

"Okay. But hurry. Like I said, I've got to get out of here."

I'd dug down about a foot when Red came back with all the rest of them. Paul Heissen and the other cops and the doctor. They wanted to take me away. But I asked Paul. He made them let me stay. I stood where I could watch. The young cops dug very rapidly.

"Look for a black tin suitcase," I told them.

But it wasn't the black tin suitcase at all. And then they took me away.

70-6-3